The Warden's Legacy

by

J.A. Giunta

Brick Cave Media
brickcavebooks.com

ISBN-13 978-1-938190-64-3

Printed in the United States of America.

The characters and events in this book are fictitious. Any similarity to real persons, living or dead, is coincidental and not intended by the author.

Cover Illustration by Henning Ludvigsen

Brick Cave Media
brickcavebooks.com

For Bob Nelson,

A good friend who works hard at making other people's dreams come true.

Also by J.A. Giunta

THE ASCENSION
Book One: *The Last Incarnation*
Book Two: *The Mists of Faeron*
Book Three: *Out of the Dark*

THE GUARDIANS
Book One: *Knights of Virtue*

TRANSCENDENT POWERS
Book One: *Supernal Dawn*

War Golem

Acknowledgements

I'd like to thank
Melissa Clazie, Sharon Skinner and Nelson Sperling
for all their help in making this book possible.

The Warden's Legacy

by

J.A. Giunta

Brick Cave Media
brickcavebooks.com

– 1 –

Stonefall opened his eyes.

Silent and still, masked nose to tail in mud, he'd caught scent of another dragon. A vague length of black and red took shape behind the eyes, as all his senses worked as one to form an image. Chill moisture in the air told of coming rains, a scent of ozone and earthen tinges, pale wind through his ears and shades of blue across his scales.

The other dragon jarred them all, overcame him with its presence in the breeze, pushed back against the hairs between each scale. It carried traces of dark soil and bricklebark in its claws, a swirl of browns that grew sharper with each beat of its wings. Peak fens and thistleroot across its belly pulsed greenish black, while the heady sweetness of a fresh kill in its maw swam in reds.

The forward thrust of its bulk pulsed in whites and grays, defined talon and tail, membrane and scale, horn and tooth, until the image in his mind was more detailed than the winged form that at last came into view.

Another male, Stone thought, *and larger than I.*

No chance of a meal, confrontation would only end in injury or death. Neither seemed appealing nor worth the risk. The craggy hillside he'd taken refuge in was hardly a prize, certainly not a lair. It had been moons since last he fed. Another day would do no harm. He decided his time was better spent searching elsewhere for a home.

At barely five winters old, Stone had been forced from his mother's lair when it came time for her to mate again. He'd been hiding from larger dragons and seeking shelter ever since. This coming winter would be his tenth.

The other moved further on downwind at a steady pace and circled left. Had he sensed another dragon, he would've surely attacked. He was searching the rocky earth and ravines for prey after all. Stone might not have been an easy kill, but he'd go a long way toward filling a belly.

The thought made his stomach tighten.

No dragon had ever died from starvation, but neither did the hunger ever cease. Those with a secure lair could choose to hibernate and wait for prey to replenish. Sadly, Stone was not one of them and a long way from the deep slumber.

He patiently waited for the other to be far enough away, and upwind for good measure, that it wouldn't take notice or give chase if it had. He pulled free of the mud, shook its weight from his wings and quickly left in the opposite direction.

He flew low to the ground to keep his scent from travelling far and in the hope of catching anything to eat. Most prey lived deep beneath the surface, hidden from keen ears or the reverberation of heavy wings. Still, they came up from time to time, to gather what little food the land could offer.

Creatures that dared the open were either difficult to take or posed a greater threat. Stone had seen all too often the remains of careless dragons. A single mistake, any injury to a wing, and even the largest of dragons became carrion.

Stone followed close the edge of craggy hillocks and deep ravines, always mindful of his surroundings, always careful to remain unseen. He expertly overturned rocks at steady intervals as he passed, listening and feeling for their echoes to return. A flash of browns might mean a delver warren, yellow gold a barrow slug, blue grays a mole or glow worm. All that came back, however, were the disheartened pangs of empty black.

A forest brushed his senses in salty gray and chilly dusk. On the other side of the nearest hill, just beyond the pallid blue of a dwindling stream, its taste lilted in hollow tones upon the wind. Like most woods, its boles were without fruit and gone to stone. Something rustled in the sounds though, a jagged edge of shadow green and noxious ebon to a point.

A wyvern?

Stone pulled up short, focused his attention and felt it pass before the trees. He was off in an instant, pushed forward with all speed and powerful thrusts that sent eddies of loose soil and small rocks billowing outward. Still low to the ground, belly scraping with each beat, he gritted teeth in anticipation of a long awaited meal. So overcome with an anxious surge of blood racing through his veins, he noticed too late the other two at either side far off in the distance.

It's an ambush! Stone growled and dripped liquid fire from his maw. *And like a fool, I fell for it.*

There was no turning back. The two were already closing in on his flank. He was larger than they but knew he stood no chance at killing all three directly. Facing off against one was entirely feasible, though not without risk. Three was simply out of the question.

While wyverns somewhat resembled small dragons, in that they had wings and talons, sharp teeth and a pointed maw, the similarities ended there. They had no scales to speak of, no horns nor spine ridges, no deadly breath of any kind, but their tails ended in a bulbous stinger with a highly potent poison. The toxin was strong enough to render any creature helpless within moments and killed from within by eating away at vital organs.

Unlike dragons, however, wyverns had imperfect perception. As with any creature that relied heavily upon sight, they could easily be tricked.

Stone sped straight for the lone wyvern and took it full on in the chest. He turned his body away at the last moment, avoided the stinger by a scales breadth and shoved the smaller creature into the stony limbs of a tree. It crashed through in a burst of bright shards and debris before tumbling tail over head toward the ground.

He followed without delay, wings tight at his side. He pulled up at the last, barely slowing his descent, and landed with great force upon the wyvern. Beneath the crushing weight, its chest collapsed to the sickly crunch of bones shattered into flesh and the torrid wetness of every organ pressed to ruin. Its tail twitched for a brief moment, but life had left its eyes.

The other two were nearly there.

Stone sighed in frustration, as his stomach knotted at the smell of meat. It would've made quite the meal, if he survived and could reach it before scavengers caught the scent. He forced regret aside and took wing deeper into the forest.

Few dragons would consider traversing the petrified trees. The density of varied trunks and webwork of clawlike limbs made it difficult to navigate, with far more risk than reward. Stone had little choice. He needed the thick boles and scattered sunlight to obscure vision, to trap his prey into thinking they were the hunters.

Ranging from fairly slender, no wider than a leg, to

truly massive in girth, some trees spanned the length of a dozen dragons end to end and were of a height to block all trace of sun and sky when viewed from below. In varied states of decay, once victims of dragon breath, some were hollowed out shells, now frozen in time, while others had borne the brunt and stood defiant in its wake. The true danger in flying between the hardened trees was in the haphazard growth of outstretched limbs. One slip in judgement, a single lapse in concentration, could mean a fatal tear in a wing or a cascade of stony timber.

An unpleasant end, either way.

Stone sensed a fallen tree up ahead, far enough off the ground for a ruse. He slowed to allow the pair within range and dove toward the log, clawing up earth as he passed beneath. One chose to fly around, while the other flew headlong into the cloud of upended dirt. Stone raked talons against the petrified wood to slow his momentum and carry him into a turn on the other side. He swooped back down with claws ready as the baited wyvern came through.

He took hold of it by neck and tail, forced its stinger to the ground and bit down at the base. Through acrid flesh and heavy muscle, knobby bone and fragile spine, Stone pulled free its wriggling tail to the ruddy gold of an anguished cry. The wound spewed a viscous black of jingling heat across his claw. Its lifeblood in his mouth, stomach clamoring for more, he once again forced down the hunger at his core.

The other wyvern had swung around, hovered in air and watched on, exuding the heady scent of ashen fear in beat and breath. Stone saw and felt the very moment realization dawned upon the creature, when it knew the chase had turned and its only option was to flee.

Stone pushed off with all strength, called up the roiling bile deep within him. Mere wingspans away, the molten longing reached his throat. It ignited in his maw, flowed between teeth and tongue, and dripped in a fiery semblance of saliva along his jaw. He loosed the stream of liquid flames with a roar that shook the trees. So hot as to warp the air around it, his breath engulfed the wyvern tail to breast.

Flesh curled and blood boiled, beneath the charring of brittle wings. A pained keen escaped its mouth, but the inferno raced inward, soon stole all from its lungs, and burned the wyvern from within. The smoking ruin of its carcass plummeted to the ground, smashed through waiting limbs amidst a shower of forest bones.

Stone quickly followed, as a nervous thrill fled his heart and unrelenting hunger moved to fore. He landed heavily upon the remains, splitting char and brittle frame in swirls of smoke. He tore open its chest and began to feed.

There was never time to savor. Meals were a frenzied race to finish before something else, something more dangerous, caught the scent. He wasted little time in chewing but gulped down each bite of charred meat, senses lost in the tender whites and ashen reds across his tongue. There were still two more wyverns. If he didn't hurry—

He sensed a pair of stalkers enter the forest.

Wisps of shadow at first, his senses sharpened their shapes into powerful creatures on all fours—sleek, agile, torrid fur in rumbling stripes of black and gold. Lethal felines the size of wyrmlings, these two were merely scouts. The cats hunted as a pride. Three times as many would be waiting beyond the trees.

Stone wasn't at all surprised but more than mildly annoyed. He'd hoped to at least start on the second wyvern before being forced to flee or carry his meal away. Both stalkers had reached the first and would soon prowl toward the next. They had an exceptional sense of smell, but neither showed sign of noting his presence.

Frustrated, barely sated, he grabbed the carcass and flew deeper into the forest, farther than any dragon should ever dare to go. The trees were without mark or scent of any kind. There was no sense of another creature, no trace of lair or den. Lifeless and still, the long dead woodland offered little but quiet dark and empty solitude.

No dragon should ever come here, Stone thought in a sardonic tone, *because there's nothing to eat. Not even a scent or sound of water.* The trees had grown larger the further in he ventured, some so wide he had no choice but to sway his course around them. He'd slowed his pace by half again to avoid being skewered by any number of jutting limbs. *This place is a deathtrap.*

A sound overtook him then, so startling he nearly dropped the only meal he'd had in moons. Both quiet and somewhat loud, like echoed whispers in his mind, they spoke a language he'd never heard—or no language at all. A shiver shook his spine, like charged talons swept across every scale and bone beneath. It seemed to lead in one direction, grew weak if he turned away to either side.

As he followed the strange whispers, the largest tree he'd ever seen came into sense. It towered over all the others, with branches that mushroomed out into a cloud cover of diffused light and shadowed grays. The face of it was like a wall, a sheer cliff of frozen wood that stretched the length of a hundred trees.

He flew into the whispers like pushing hard against a current. Its lull beckoned, pulled him forward, but the power trembling through his middle warned him to turn away. He landed before the great tree, where the echoes were strongest, and left behind his prized meal for a closer look.

He sensed an opening in the tree his eyes couldn't

see, one widened by hand and edges smoothed as eroded stone. He thumped the ground with his tail, sensed clearly in the vibrations some illusion at work, a play of light simple vision could not confirm.

Is this magic?

He'd only heard of it in tales his mother told, stories of fantastic battles fought to safeguard their future, when the dragons of old had faced down a blight upon the world, had scoured all with breath and claw until not a single foe remained.

There hasn't been magic, Stone thought, *since the time of the Wardens.*

Or so he'd been taught.

Could his mother have been wrong? He reached a claw out to the false breach. Could their enemies yet live? He pushed past without resistance into the cold of a hollowed bole. Then why haven't they restored the trees they so revered before their fall?

Stone quieted his racing mind and stepped through the absent opening, into the vacant tree, onto a floor that was not there.

It was difficult to gauge how long he'd been falling, tumbling head over tail down the narrow passage. What wasn't hard to sense, despite his initial shock and subsequent disorientation, was the mass of lengthy spikes rushing up to greet him.

Stone flung wide both arms and legs, dug deep each talon into either wall, and slowed his descent to a shower of silver sparks. The gouges deepened to the first knuckle before he came to a complete stop, suspended upside down and eyes a hair length from pointed iron. A long moment passed before he could breathe again, when the pounding in his chest had subsided to a steady throb.

Further up the fashioned tunnel was another set of echoed whispers, an opening on his left hid by illusion.

He carefully relaxed his legs and let fall his bottom half so he could turn and face upward without being marred. He was tempted to breathe the iron into a puddle of slag but wanted more to be away and back on solid footing.

As he passed through the second opening, he found it easier to differentiate between the whispers far above, those just behind him and the ones emanating from an egg at the center of the chamber.

It was unlike any he'd seen before, too small to be a dragon and too thick to be a wyvern. The shell had no spots or dimples, no speckles or grooves, just a patterned wave of striations like eddies in muddied water. Smooth, almost polished, it had the semblance of tree rings, though wider at the middle and warped along the lines. The whispers came from the shell itself, not whatever grew inside.

Stone thumped his tail against the floor and was puzzled by the egg's shape. He tapped the shell with a talon and caught glimpses of arms and legs. Another tap showed no tail and a rounded head with rounded ears.

It can't be. He wondered, *Can it?*

He rapped against the shell until he sensed every facet of the creature's form, every curve and fleshy fold. He realized it was unlike any he'd seen before, because one like it had not been seen in generations.

Encased in Warden magic, it was a being the world had lived without for a thousand turns. For all he knew, it was the only one of its kind, the last of its kind. Remnant of a species now thought to be extinct, it should've perished long ago in the fires of dragon breath.

The egg Stone had found wasn't merely unusual or even rare...

It was *human.*

– 2 –

Stone scratched at the egg with a talon, traced each striation, but was unable to mar the glossy surface. No matter how hard he pushed, the odd shell resisted and wouldn't be pierced. There was no doubt Warden magic made it stronger.

Why even open it? he wondered, still searching for a weakness. *Whatever's inside is long dead.*

No heartbeat meant no meal. What other reasons then remained? Curiosity? The need to put a face on the villains of their stories? He'd never encountered magic before, only heard of it in tales. The creature inside could be dangerous.

He considered the whispers. Were they alive? Could they be reasoned with? Did they serve a purpose apart from protecting the egg? What if it was they who were driving him to break the shell, to set loose their hidden weapon and exact revenge from beyond death?

Could they be fooled?

Stone placed a palm over the egg, spread his warmth and echoed beat all throughout. Eyes closed and head raised, he spoke in what he hoped sounded a solemn tone.

"I will safeguard this child with my life."

Moments passed in silence. When nothing happened, he peaked with one eye. The egg remained the same. He gave a sigh and attributed the silly attempt to fanciful tales told by his mother.

"It was a worth a try, I suppose."

A beat pulsed within the egg.

Stone snatched his hand away as if he'd been bitten. He thumped his tail in a short rhythm and studied closer what lay inside. The human was still. It drew no breath nor had a heartbeat, though he was certain he'd just felt one. What if it was in a sort of hibernation? Cautiously, he put his palm back. The deep slumber could resemble death—

The beat resounded once again.

It's alive!

Excited, he began searching anew for a way to crack the shell. He leaned forward and took the egg into his mouth. With practiced care, he bit down in growing strength. He wanted inside without spilling its contents on the floor.

Despite his best efforts, the shell wouldn't break. If the egg was any smaller, he'd have risked swallowing it whole. It'd eventually come apart in his stomach, at least he hoped.

He let out a deep breath in frustration that sent curls of flame across its surface. Something within the egg caught his attention, a thin layer of rowed empty space on the other side. He rolled the egg over and heard within the rows prickled circles and slender lengths. The whispers had kept them hidden, in illusion and clever placement.

More flame and thumping showed the access, small holes in a spread of five. Stone depressed one with a talon. It opened a scant depth, barely half a scale. The others lined up like the ends of a hand. Not the hand of a dragon but a human's.

Stone pressed in the tips of four talons and another from his left hand, a difficult task for one his size. When nothing seemed to happen, no matter how hard he pushed, he tried moving his claw to a more comfortable position. A circular section of shell began to turn. He continued the motion and sensed within the shell a movement of its delicate parts.

The prickled circles moved within a groove, and the slender lengths slid one along the other. He felt and heard a click just as a seam appeared lengthwise across the center of the egg.

Air escaped in a faint rush, like the exhalation of an anxious breath. It held the bitter greens and biting whites of blossomed life and blooming bough, the caress of sweet blues in summer wind and dulcet yellows in rays of sun. Its touch was so clean, so pure within his lungs, that he coughed in the face of it and longed for more when it was gone.

The egg's magic had fled.

Left behind were perfect halves, interlocking edges of shell fashioned to fit without a flaw. Stone lifted the top and set it aside, revealing the human child now cradled on its back. Heady soil spilled out on either side, like a rainfall of dark and crumbled past. The human had been encased in it, a seed planted long ago in an egg that would never hatch.

As with the openings in the tree and long passage sloping down, the egg had been shaped—was no egg at all. Another illusion, another trick, it served more than a single purpose. It protected the child, kept it hidden from harm, but also fooled the unwary into setting it free. The words played out in Stone's mind over and again, as he looked down on the species that had wreaked havoc upon the world.

"What have I done?"

The child drew a breath, tightened its eyes and began to cry. Hands balled into little fists, feet kicking in the air, body trembling in the soil, the feared enemy of all dragons wailed on without end. How such a frail and tiny creature was meant to survive was beyond Stone. It had no claws to fight with, no teeth to rend flesh, no hide for protection. It'd even begun to wheeze and sputter on its own breath, as if the very air sought to end such a fragile existence.

Stone worried its noisome cries might attract the pride of stalkers, even from this distance. His curiosity sated, there was no need of further risk. He opened his maw and reached out for the child. A mere breath from its flesh, the most extraordinary thing happened.

Shoots began to sprout up from the soil.

Tiny and curled, a drawn flow of melodic greens, they pushed through dark earth from beneath the child's hands. Tufts of fibrous moisture, both patches exuded the cloying brush of springtime rains and spread along their lengths into the slight span of budding leaves. The sense of it all left him stunned in wondrous silence.

Plant life was uncommon. Some beautiful to behold, others dangerous and deceptive, all were a prized treat for those few strong enough to claim its yield. Stone had never been this close, had only sensed it from a distance, where its touch was just allure. To see and feel it grow before him, to hear its hurried pace, was more than just fantastic.

It was magical.

He lifted the child between the blunted undersides of two talons and placed it in a rounded corner of exposed earth and rocky root. Ignoring the incessant cries and faltered wheezing, Stone returned to the half shell. He watched closely the new shoots, but to his surprise and dismay, nothing more seemed to happen.

He stirred and prodded at the soil, upending fresh buds and their coiled tips. Confused and a bit annoyed, he couldn't understand why they'd stopped growing. He waited patiently for some time, worried he'd somehow ruined them.

It was only when the child's cries had grown much stronger that Stone decided he'd had enough. He turned to end the mewling creature but gave pause at what he saw.

Moss spread up from the child's hand along a root now brown as earth. Leaves and shoots sprang from the other, the beginnings of a vine. He saw eddies in the air, the same purity and potence as what had surged from out the egg. He also noticed though the child continued wailing, no longer did it wheeze.

It was the child, he realized, that'd caused the plants to grow. He lifted it back up with care and placed it in the bed of soil. The human was now too important to be made a meal, for Stone or any other.

Suddenly, it was possible to return the world to how it was, to thriving forests filled with life and fertile fields awash in color. To the time before dragons had set it all aflame.

Despite the hope that swelled Stone's breast, the child cried out with every breath.

"Perhaps that's what I should call you," Stone said amidst the din. "Crier."

* * *

Rain had made it difficult to find prey, colored senses with its clamor and downpour of vibrations. Stone had shed his scales twice since on his own, and though he'd learned to isolate perceptions in all that time, it was still a struggle to rely on any one without the others.

Day began to fade before he finally relented. There would be no meal that day, not for the human child. He'd considered checking the fallen wyverns but knew it a lost cause. There'd been no sign of the pride when he circled wide the surrounding trees, before heading out in search of food. They wouldn't have left the forest without taking the other two.

The third had provided a small respite, but his fiery attack had left precious little to feast upon. When he'd eaten all he could, Stone crushed and burned the body further to eliminate all scent. He'd slept within the great tree a short distance away, to be certain no stalkers had followed after.

And how am I to feed it? Stone thought of the frail creature he'd left behind. *I can barely feed myself.*

The mantra came to him unbidden, words his mother had often spoke.

Kill. Feed. Grow.

Far easier said than done, the haunting melody of her tone played on along his spine, grating every nerve with sullen failure. Four winters come and gone, with him scarcely a scale larger and arguably little wiser. It made him wonder how many lives had gone to fueling her goodly size.

He wasn't even sure what meal was suited to a toothless child. Milk, he supposed, though the odds of finding prey to produce it seemed slim to none. Not to mention the minor obstacle of procuring it from a teat. That wasn't something he could manage on his own.

What was he to do then, capture a new mother for the child to suckle on?

I could always chew for him, Stone surmised, as he flew back into the forest. *Assuming I ever find another meal...*

He'd entered at the other end of the trees, had fully searched their considerable expanse earlier in the day and found nothing to show for his pains. Nothing grew in the forest but shadow and disappointment.

Not that he'd had any more luck in the hills and low mountains. What little grass he'd seen was brittle yellow and brown decay, picked clear before the coming of new winter. Any tracks he caught sense of trailed off into the earth, in deep burrows and warrens no dragon could reach. More than one cave offered promise of feeble hope but delivered shattered bones and faded sign.

His task might've been easier had he not been forced to fly between claimed stretches of marked lairs. He'd reached none of the other dragons in size, nor could he risk them if he had. Much more was at stake now than his belly or a home.

The child had somehow caused plants to grow by touch alone. In that moment, Stone had made a choice. He'd keep the child safe, put its needs above his own. Which meant he had to be careful, even more so than usual. If he died, the child would soon follow and with it any hope of a second chance.

Dragons had burned the world, but one would also put it right.

Stone reared up within the storm.

The pride came into sense, a whirling musk of damp coats and prickled rumbles. Nine in all, they prowled near the base of the great tree. Even from this distance and through the rain, Crier could be heard, an echoed wail of fearful white.

He needed to decide, in that moment, what he'd give, what he was willing to sacrifice for the child and any hope at restoring all the forests. His death benefited no one, but would he risk wing or limb? Risk the unending pain and diminished strength that came of wounds?

Nothing less than an elder dared face a full pride. Dragons fought head on, killed quickly and fed. Much like he'd faced the three wyverns, he'd need a different strategy to survive.

Wing to wind, Stone flew as fast as he could manage, slipped past bole and bough without a sound or scent to mark him. The storm blew all trace of him behind, carried it away in the whistling snaps and gray rush of its embrace.

Each one distinct in his mind, he tracked their every pace, every paw in sucking mud and claw scrape against rock. They spoke wordlessly to one another, purred and growled their intent. Their numbers spread like a talon, the two in front had reached the whispers of a wall that wasn't there.

Stone grabbed hold of a thick limb as he soared past, held tight a broken length in each claw as the pride turned. Too late to act, let alone give breath to warning, the furthest cat from the tree caught both broken pieces in its chest.

Liquid fire preceded Stone, a great gust of grisly bile that clung and burned through all it touched. The pride was forced apart and into the trees. He swooped down and snatched one up, without breaking stride or stream. It fought against his clutch, twisted in his grasp. Though it clawed away scales, bit into his flesh, the damage was minimal. The wounds would heal and his scales return with his next molt.

He landed in the small clearing, in the flames that fought and hissed against the rain. The stalker underfoot mewled its pain in panicked cries, scrabbled to break free as mane and maw gave way to fire. Stone eyed those that remained with disdain and deadly challenge, met each pair of golden fury with an ire all his own.

The largest of them snarled and leapt, claw to fore, into the fire. Batted aside by a swift wing, it was met with a fresh stream of unforgiving breath. Though its massive paw had scraped along the outer ridge, even managed to tear away a wing talon, it had failed to maim by piercing the fragile membrane. Burned and bitter, the alpha scrambled back into a tree.

The stalker in Stone's clutch no longer cried.

He saw confusion and desperation, as he searched for his next. No doubt he was the first dragon to ever face them with such guile and disregard.

First, Stone thought, as he noted the scarred back leg of a smaller female, *and last.*

The old injury limited her speed and motion. If she'd carried milk, he would've saved her for last. Instead, he marked her with a snoutful of air and leapt away from the broken body.

Another dragon would've fed and been glad for the meal, though few would've considered eating an entire pride. Stone turned into the storm and let it carry him back. He fought now for more than hunger and couldn't hazard their survival. If even one should escape, there was no telling if it would return.

He took the female and burned another as he passed between the trees. Higher and higher he went, before setting her loose with some force. She careened through the air, destined to land on all fours but not withstand such a height. If stony limbs didn't kill her, the sudden stop surely would.

Down to five, the pride scattered. Stone hunted each one and brought their corpses to the great tree. He fed until his stomach could hold no more, waited in the rain and ate again.

Crier went through bouts of wailing, interspersed with quiet sleep. Stone pulled free one of the skulls and cleansed it with fire. He held it to a stalker and let its essence pool within. Though he hadn't been able to find the child milk, he had to feed it all the same.

Blood would have to do.

* * *

The hidden chamber had changed.

Stone could sense it as he entered the tree and left behind the crackling drone of thunderous rain. Sticky yellows and sweet warmth, heady rinds and new vines, the whispered growth was enough to steal his breath. Still they went on, the hushed voices in his mind, as he cautiously slid down the tunnel. These were different from both illusions, less persistent, unsure, like the tentative steps of a hatchling. By the time he reached the bottom, he was convinced the magic came from Crier. Whether or not it was intentional, however, he had no way to be sure.

He let fall the skull in numbed surprise, spattered its contents across moss and broad leaves. Water dripped from the ceiling, along lengths of fresh vines. Interwoven and mottled with their own stalks and speckled buds, they stretched across and down walls then back into the earth through exposed holes in renewing wood. No longer the salty sting of old stones and tree bones, the great bole was returning to supple life from within. Sap and moisture commingled in rings around the pulp, down the bulb and fragrant crisp of ripe fruit.

The stem snapped as he pulled it free, sprayed dew across his fingers in an echo of chill notes. Larger than the child but much smaller than his claw, its flesh had a stippled roughness and curved bottom of some weight. Stone pierced it with a talon and drew a bead of snowy nectar.

A halting touch upon the tongue brought his hairs to

a joyed shiver. He'd never felt such fragrant tones in pale waves across his mind, such vibrance like summer sweet or rays of dulcet through his middle. One bite and then another, its song was gone in fading whites. If not for the already mounting pressure in his belly, he would've gone for the rest and eaten all in short time.

Wailing pushed its way once more to the fore.

"Right," Stone said to his unhappy ward. "I very nearly forgot." He plucked another fruit and pierced its flesh. "Here we go."

A gentle squeeze and the first drop touched Crier's lips. Only moments more of crying went by before a pause, when tearful eyes blinked and his mouth closed for a startled taste. Too slow with another drop, Stone was met with a second bout.

"Alright, alright." Each drop seemed a surprise. "How about this?" Stone held the fruit to Crier's lips and let the child suckle. "There we go. Much better now."

It'd been so long since before the wailing, he could still feel memory of it in his ears. Though the room was far from quiet, it was finally at peace.

This fruit, Stone thought, *was all his doing. The child made it grow, along with all these others.* He slipped his tail around a vine, gave a pull and found it sturdy. *Is this what the world was like?*

His mother's stories did little justice, to the varied plants and vivid sense, nor did she capture the haunting wonder or nervous joy he'd found in magic. Granted, she'd only passed on what she'd been told when she was young.

If food like this grew, why did they burn it all away? Some of the old dragons yet lived, lost to deep slumber. He could ask them, if he could find them, though he imagined they'd sooner feast on his corpse than answer his questions. *To flush humans out from hiding?* Stone shook his head at the careless waste. *Perhaps they thought it would grow back, as it surely must've always done before.* No one knew it had been the Wardens that made the forests flourish. His mother certainly hadn't. *And if they did,* he wondered but sadly knew the answer, *would they still have killed every last human once the Wardens were no more?*

Dragons could eat fruit, but they craved flesh and blood. They may not have realized destroying their only enemy put their own food at risk, that without the forests and its bounty, everyone would starve.

Stone looked about the chamber, at the budding fruit and verdant growth, at life returning to the tree.

"And where there's food..."

His mind began to race, at worries real and then imagined. Other dragons would come, as well as a host of lesser creatures he'd be hard pressed to defend against. How was he to protect Crier without risking the child's life?

Leaving was no better than staying. At least here, they had food. The great tree provided shelter, and they were hidden fairly well—for the moment, anyway. He'd need more than tooth and claw to safeguard both their lives.

He gave the vines another pull.

No, if he wasn't large enough or strong enough to fend off other dragons, he'd have to think of another way.

– 3 –

True to his name, Crier cried. A lot.

It wasn't enough to keep him fed, Stone learned as the days passed. The child easily grew cold, shivered in seeming spasms and changed colors at the tips. His coat was hairless and delicate, overly sensitive and too weak to retain any warmth. Stone tried covering him in soil and blankets of moss, but neither were enough to fend off the chill. In the end, he brought small stones down to the chamber and placed them in the egg in a circle about its edge. It took great care to heat them without touching Crier's skin, for even the slightest lick of flame caused him damage.

Even warm, the child found cause to complain. It wanted to be kept dry at all times, no easy task for a creature that wept without end and lacked the strength or will to leave its shell. Especially when said creature emptied bowel and bladder where it slept.

"Honestly," Stone told him, as he picked feces from the soil, "I don't think your kind was meant to survive."

The child couldn't walk, Stone discovered when he'd tried to help. Its little legs were too weak and wobbly to balance such an odd shape. It had no motion at all, just laid there on its belly and cried at the sudden cold.

Neither could it hunt, though without teeth or claws, that really wasn't a wonder. Content to suckle fruit, it was still unable to feed itself. Utterly helpless, without defense, fragile and impossibly small, it needed constant attention and immense patience on his part.

"What would you do without me?"

Crier squealed and smiled wide.

* * *

Over time, Stone observed and dealt with whatever upset the child, though he had difficulties of his own. Shortly after he'd finally digested the entire pride, he was overcome with the tingling pressure and tight onset of a molt. He'd needed more room than the chamber afforded but refused to go far. With help from surrounding trees, he'd slipped free his old scales and was forced to wait while the new ones hardened.

The great tree had changed as well, returned to life at a steady pace. From chamber to roots and up toward the base, its stone softened and breathed as creaking wood once again.

Stone had taken to clearing away all the vines from the chamber. They grew too far and fast for his liking and sought to choke the other plants. It was challenging enough to move his bulk about the egg without catching wing or horn in their grasp. Luckily, he'd found a use for them, a way to keep their home safe, though more often than not he thought of leaving.

His greater size made traversing the tunnel easier, but caring for Crier in the chamber less so. They'd need to move before another molt, before the chamber was out of reach.

Still, even with him removing vines every morn, he'd find one in Crier's grasp when he returned. The way the child looked at it and made noises in a semblance of speech, it seemed as if the two were conversing. As silly as that seemed, Stone was glad for any distraction that kept Crier from crying. There was work to be done, and soothing the child between sleep was a task he could do without.

The moon had grown full by the time Stone was content with his traps. It was difficult to fool a dragon, to hide danger in a ruse. The only way to trick perfect sense was to offer no trick at all.

High above the forest floor, hanging from the great tree's limbs, were hundreds of stony pieces tied by vines. A deadly shower in wait, not all were meant to fall. Only Stone knew which vines, wrapped around every tree, would set loose the few. Meant to maim or even kill, they were the advantage he needed to face a larger foe.

Or so he hoped.

Half asleep within the chamber, his body wrapped around the egg, Stone dreaded thought of leaving but considered where to go. Soon the great tree would be a beacon, drawing creatures to its fruit. Their blood, once he'd slain them, would in turn attract dragons.

We'd have to leave the forest, he reasoned, *though which way to go from here?*

He'd been moving toward the Wall since he left his mother's lair. Whether out of morbid curiosity or an inner wish for his own end, he only knew no other dragon would dare go there.

We could return to an empty cave. A temporary solution, but lairs were hard to come by. He'd been searching for one all his adult life. *Or the cavern—*

He caught sense of a strange creature, one that moved too fast to form an image beyond the glimpse of limbs and wings. Small, upright, it darted between the trees, disappeared entirely and reappeared moments later a good distance away. Time and again, the creature vanished and reemerged, speeding on like a spirit, but when it finally came to a brief rest, it resembled a winged human.

A female.

She stopped outside the great tree, just a tail length from the hidden entrance. Much larger than Crier, her wings were translucent, rushing violets and spotted blues amidst a pattern of black lines and a blacker edge. She bore the sallow reek of a shroomden, even carried the spores upon her. Whatever underground warren she'd come from, it was a place of dank walls, muddied ground and soured air. All clung to her frame like a miasma.

She put a hand against the tree, dropped down to her knees and tilted back her head with a sharp intake of breath.

Stone was up and in the tunnel without delay, propelled himself forward by wing and claw. She must've heard and broke off. She was gone before he could reach the surface, had disappeared into the night with only a trace of her passage. A fading streamer of magic in her wake, like a dying whisper in the dark, it seemed to promise that soon she'd be back.

* * *

Crier's sense had become blinding.

Scent of his waste overpowered all else, despite Stone carrying away any feces. The soil had held and shared its memory of abuse and returned the ill favor with a rash. Not only did the child need to be kept warm and dry, it seemed, but apparently required frequent cleaning. It had no way to lick itself, and like assistance was out of the question. Stone knew what the child slept in. He'd sooner bite off his own tongue than press it to the boy's skin.

This meant regular outings to a nearby puddle left by rain. Stone had deepened the depression since first dipping Crier in and had later filled its bottom with rocks. A few moments of fiery breath had left a hardened slag, which prevented water seeping into the earth. Now whenever one was needed, a bath was always at hand.

The child's puffy, reddened bottom hadn't improved right away, which led Stone to suspect the muddied rainwater wouldn't do. Fortunately, the more he soaked Crier within the puddle, the clearer it became. Whether the impurities had dissipated or the child's touch had been the cause, Stone was merely glad for the return to relative quiet.

He'd been replacing the egg's soil every morning, was carrying it back when he heard the whispers once again. They were fainter than the illusions, as if at a distance or in hiding. Unlike the tingling echoes in his mind, this magic chilled his every sense with the subtle colors of a breeze.

He last saw the other human a moon ago but had felt eyes upon him ever since.

"I know you're there," he said into the wind, into the rustle of dust and breath. Nothing but swirling blues and the reverberation of his own heartbeat answered back. "There's nothing here for you."

Stone waited long moments in chilling quiet and empty wind.

Crier cried out.

A frustrated sigh, and Stone was back into the tree. He returned the egg to its place and set Crier in its soil. The child gave a sharp laugh and cooed a dribbling trill.

"Glad to see me?" Stone asked, as he put back the

ring of warming rocks. “Are you hungry?” Crier looked up with a wordless query and set wide his toothless smile. “I’ll take that as a yes.”

Once Crier was fed and settled, he shook with a little yawn. Stone had learned to wait for that moment, when tiny fingers no longer grabbed at the hairs of his chin, when tired eyelids opened more and more slowly before resigning to fall asleep and the small stretch of a jaw grew to steady, calm breath.

Normally, he’d curl his length about the egg and fall to sleep as well, but the nagging presence wouldn’t leave. Its whispers and watching eyes had grown bold with the full moon.

Stone returned to the forest floor.

“What is it you want?” he demanded of the air. He might as well have been talking to spirits. Nothing was within sense but the persistent aura of a being. “Leave this place while still you can.”

He sensed her before she spoke, the human stepping from the tree’s shadow.

“What are you hiding, I wonder.” Her voice was sure, unafraid despite the danger. No further did she move, kept one foot in shadow. “So unusual for your kind.”

“And you?” Stone asked, looked down on the small creature and moved his tail within range. “Are you unusual for your kind?”

Her snort of laughter was without mirth.

“Very.”

Her eye twitched and head tilted to the side, almost as if in pleasure. Hand flat against the tree, she began to vibrate in nearly undiscernible waves of violet and coarse quivers.

She’s feeding, Stone realized, could sense the great tree fade from wood to stone beneath her touch. *Could she too be a Warden?*

"Stop," he warned in a level tone, tensed his body and claws to strike. "You're killing that tree."

"Isn't that what you want?" The patch of stone began to spread. "If not, you should. I felt life within the forest. Others will too."

Stone leapt, but she was gone, a mere slip across his claws. He felt the whispers rise within him in the instant her body faded. She'd disappeared from reach, shrank into shadow and the nothingness of violet whispers, but her magic still lingered. He followed their sense of shifting chill and rolling dark beneath the ground, traced its path within the shade and saw its aim.

Stone swiped out with his tail as she reached a patch of sunlight between the trees. She appeared as he'd expected, slipped out from the shadow like rippling water in the air. He knocked her back, against a tree, not hard enough to kill but enough to leave her dazed. With only a moment to consider, to thwart a creature that moved through darkness, Stone snatched her up between two talons by a layer of loose flesh and held her aloft within the sun.

"If you disappear once more," he fairly growled and called up bile to his throat, "I'll burn you and every tree in your path into the ground."

Her eyes fluttered open, like painful waking from a dream.

"Of course you will," she said and groaned. A trail of crimson humming ran from a gash upon her forehead. Angry and a bit frantic, she added, "Isn't that what dragons do? Burn it all and damn the consequence?"

The way she squirmed within his grasp made him realize she was adorned. Whatever he'd gripped her by was wrapped about her like a second skin.

"What is this?" he asked and poked at the strange material. "And why do you hide yourself within it?"

She looked about for any shadow and found none within her reach. Though she bore a brave demeanor, he sensed a budding fear beneath the anger and sullen bluster.

"It's clothing, you daft lizard. Woven garment from spider silk." With a grumble, she gave up wriggling. "I wear it to keep warm and for protection. How did you know where I was? Nothing, not even a dragon, has ever seen me move through shadow."

Clever, Stone admitted of the clothing. Such a thing would've been helpful in dealing with Crier these past moons. *Still could be.*

"Not see," he told her, studied how the garment was positioned about her body. "I sensed your magic, when you disappeared and moved." A female would've been convenient as well, though this one had no milk. "I'd never heard of humans, not even Wardens, who were possessed of such a power."

The fold above her eyes had crinkled.

"That's not possible," she said, as if talking not to him but to herself. "You can't hear magic. Can you?" A shake of her head, and her eyes were directed at him again. "I suppose you need me for something." Stone narrowed his eyes. "Otherwise you would've killed me? So, what is it then?"

"Where have you come from?" She wasn't entirely like Crier, though no more different than some dragon lines were from another. "How many more of you are there?"

Her wings brushed against his scales with every nervous flutter. It was possible Crier was too young to have sprouted his yet, just as his head had little hair, while this one's was down to past her middle, with gathered strands tied and interwoven. Her ears were very different from his as well, so long they swept back past her head and to a taper. In many ways, she was more draconic than like the child.

"I come from nowhere," she replied, dark eyes cold and hardened by troubled thought. Her skin was also far paler, with a faint shimmer like starlight song. "And there is no one in the world quite like me."

"You evade my questions, human?" He shook her for good measure. "I may yet kill you all the same."

"You think I'm human?" she asked with incredulity, her tone just short of mocking laughter. "The only one of those left in existence is the Warden you've got stowed away."

Stone drew her in closer, his belly seething with a sudden ire.

"What would you know of Wardens?"

She crossed her arms in defiance, despite the spreading pit of dread within her sense.

"Enough to know they were all dead," she replied, "killed by dragons years ago. All the humans were."

He'd never heard the word before and wondered what length of time it marked. Humans had been wiped out more than a thousand cycles ago.

Perhaps humans measure time in larger scale. Maybe by generation? Then again, this one seems to claim she isn't human.

She went on, "That's why the trees are dead. Or they were." She looked back to the great tree. "Where did you find him? More importantly," she asked and met his withering gaze, "why'd you let him live? Why are you raising him like your own?"

She posed more questions than answers, and Stone began to weary of the exchange.

"You said I should want the great tree dead."

"To stay hidden," she explained. "It's the baby that makes it live again, yes? So, if I feed on it, keep its growth in check, no one else would be drawn here."

That would actually solve a looming problem, Stone thought. By her smile, she knew it too.

"Give me your garment."

She blinked. "What?"

"Remove the clothing and give it to me." She took so long to comply, he decided to lend assistance. "How does it come off?"

"Hey!" She slapped at his talon but in no way deterred his course. "These aren't exactly easy to come by! Well, they are, but it's *really* inconvenient." He kept trying to find a way to pull it loose. "Oh, fine!"

She pulled an end from beneath a loop at her waist, unrolled it from her body and remained fluttering in air. The garment was a single length, like a flattened worm. She hovered nearby as he studied and tested its strength.

"Do we have a deal then?" she asked, arm covering her breasts and other hand over a nether spot. Her cheeks had also brightened with sudden flush. "Can I feed without you trying to kill me?"

Try? He gave her a dubious look.

"Yes," he agreed, "but stay away from the child. If I ever find you near him, our accord and your life are at an end."

It was her turn to make a face.

"Agreed." She considered a moment. "What do I call you? My name's Glimmershin Suncaller."

"Stonefall," he said and wrapped the garment about a talon. "You may call me Stone."

"Great! You can call me Glimmershin Suncaller."

There was a playful twist to her lips, as if she tried to gauge his humor.

"Alright," he said and headed back for the great tree, "Glim."

"Glimmershin," she yelled after. "Suncaller."

"Goodbye, Glim."

With a short laugh, she flew away.

– 4 –

The charred bitter snap of fired shroomden, the gray pall of ground haircap, the lasting clamor of fetid blackroot, a vile cacophony of sour sweat and the acrid stains of turned soil, Glim had returned days later with all manner of sense upon her.

Stone sat in the muted colors of calm and quiet outside the tree, his mind upon the wind and the child lost to sleep. He'd grown to cherish such moments and refused to let the outcry of her presence drown them out.

He noticed she'd been cautiously feeding on the upper bole and branches, so as not to spoil the chamber fruits. The depleted wood beneath her touch became as stone, petrified like all the others.

It wasn't dragonfire after all, he'd thought, *though I'm sure we played a part. The trees may have burned, along with humans and their cities, but it was* her *kind that had killed off all the forests.*

There was a measure of lessened guilt, a trifle comfort in the thought. As with most things in life, he took it without complaint. Stone considered any ease beyond survival to be a boon.

"Tell me," he said and opened his eyes to sunlight song, "if you're not human, what are you?"

Glim finished with an exhalation of content, flew over and sat beside him. She wore a new garment, the sweet pale of fresh rain and gray rancor of a warren.

"I'm fey."

"You said you're unlike others of your kind." He looked over at her tiny form, barely the length of a talon, and wondered just how much she differed. "Do all feys feed on trees and disappear into the dark?"

He wasn't sure if her hesitation stemmed from painful memory or words carefully chosen.

"We do...*did* feed on trees," she said, pulled knees to her chest and wrapped both arms about them. "We live underground now and feed on shroomdens." By her tone at the last, she found no pleasure in the massive stalks. "They grow far and tall but taste like rotted earth. They don't sustain quite the same as trees or plants, either. With the trees...it's like, I can taste the sunlight running through them." She smiled at the thought, but it soon faded to pursed lips. "Shroomdens crowd over one another and rain their spores over everything, until they're all I can smell. And they're grit gets into everything!"

"Did you live here, in the forest?" It'd been so long since he spoke, had a real conversation, that he hadn't realized how much he missed it—how much he missed... her. "Not you, your kind."

"No, I lived here. When I was young." She looked up into the skeleton of old forest bones, as if she saw them as they were, bristling with leaf and life. "That's why I come here sometimes. It reminds me who I am, that I'm not just what I was born as. I'm all the things I've done and all I've yet to do."

It was difficult not to think of her as a child. Her size was misleading, belied the words of subtle wisdom and lessons hard won in short time. Still, she seemed to keep too many truths to herself.

"What of the rest?"

Glim shook her head. "As far as I know, I'm the only Shadow Walker left alive." Under her breath, she added, "The conclave's seen to that."

By her demeanor, Stone surmised the claim to be neither boastful nor worthy of desire. She had the weary mien of one both hunted and haunted. It reminded him of being cast from his mother's lair.

"If they knew," she said and caught his eyes within the worry of her own, "they'd come for the child. And there's nothing you or I could do to stop them."

Stone knew it wasn't a leveled threat but a fear she was loath to fathom, as if her fate could befall Crier.

She cares for him. Momentarily suspicious, he could only wonder why. *Is feeding on the tree so important? Or is her life filled with such misery she wouldn't wish it on another?*

"We'd leave before that."

"We?" Glim asked, her gloom parted by surprise.

Stone closed his eyes and turned away, let his mind slip back into the embrace of a melodic breeze and ray of warmth between the clouds. Would he bring along the fey? She'd proved to serve a purpose, and he didn't wholly dislike the company.

"We," he said finally, his meaning still obscure.

* * *

Crier had been fed, washed and wiped, his garment rinsed, dried and wrapped about him, the egg emptied and cleaned, its soil replaced, and all trace of hanging vine cleared from the chamber. After a short time at play, to a pleasantly drawn out rumble, his eyelids began to droop and finally closed into slumber.

Stone stayed for a while, body curled about the egg. He breathed warmth back into the ring of rocks to fend off the growing chill. With persistent rains and shrinking daylight, winter would be soon upon them.

Long nights and ice aside, he'd often thought fondly on the season. It marked another cycle of his life and reminded him of home. Not all his memories were good ones, but those that were gave him comfort. Especially those—

He sensed Glim step from the shadows above and rose to greet her. The great tree had not yet recovered enough for feeding, but she'd been visiting all the same.

Sometimes he wondered if she left at all.

"Good afternoon," she said in air with what she'd told him was a curtsy—supposedly a show of respect, but her playful mien seemed more like mischief.

"To you as well," he said.

Stone began to walk toward a trail his bulk had forged over time. Glim hovered beside him, kept pace as they talked.

"Have you given it more thought?"

She'd asked if she could make a home high up in the great tree, that feys were never meant for the dank and dark of underground.

There are hundreds of trees here, he thought. *Why live in this one?* Except for the fact it was her only source of food, or at least her favorite, by far the largest and most stable, set firm at the forest's center, she seemed to want something more. *To be near Crier? I'd never allow it. Near me?* Stone shook his head. It made more sense she'd want to ensure her survival. *In her own way, she might think she's protecting the child.*

"Our agreement would still stand," he said. "You're to stay away from Crier."

Glim nodded and smiled, as if she already knew.

"Of course," she agreed. "Unless you asked me."

Stone stopped of a sudden, spine ridges flared. He'd caught sense of another dragon take shape, and a large one at that. It was already in the forest and headed their way.

"Or, no. Never," Glim said quickly. "Not even then."

"You need to hide," he told her and fought down the urge not to do the same. "Now!"

Glim disappeared into shadow.

His every instinct surged his body toward action, to flee without delay or fight to the bitter end. He'd never let urges rule him, always reasoned every recourse. This time, however, there was more at risk than just his life. There wasn't room for consideration, only a readied plan and the steeled nerve to see it through.

He turned and dashed for the clearing, claws tearing into earth and wings thrusting him forward. He turned again and spun an arc of upended soil, as the other landed on all fours with enough force to shake the ground. Spread wide and body taut, it stood easily twice his size.

"She said you'd be here," the other growled, a blackened tenor that scraped the scale. His look was both wild with the confident lust of a predator at advantage and slightly wary, if not amused, that his prey had stood its ground. "I expected to give chase. What a wonderful surprise!"

She? Does he mean Glim? Fire raged within his belly. *Has she betrayed us?*

Stone said nothing in return. There wasn't any point. Words would neither win the fray nor sway it in his favor. As well, his breath against such a larger dragon would be merely a mild annoyance. Instead he lowered his head to one side and faced the other dragon, so his neck ridges flared to protect a vital artery. He began to circle the greater foe in a methodical, slow pace. Keenly aware of his surroundings, he needed only a few more steps in either direction.

"What are you about?" the other asked.

His ears twitched and tail thumped, surveying the immediate area. He had longer horns that spiraled out in acrid greens and deeper eye ridges half-ringed in sallow spurs. His scales were flared at both sides, which left rows of sharp ridges rather than spaces between the black. Broad chestplates and a thick neck, curved barbs at every joint, it wasn't a wonder he'd survived to grow so large.

Despite their difference in bulk and reach, the other dragon began to move in a swirl of colored tremors.

Stone continued on, feigning measured preparation to attack. His mark was nearly met.

"Are you crazed?" the other asked. "So starved with delirium that you think you could best me?" Stone's recalcitrant silence was drawing ire. "Enough of this nonsense!"

He moved to strike as Stone swept a wing ridge clean through a set of vines. The other's attack came up short, stopped midway in alarm at the sense of sudden danger. Stone cut through a second set and rolled aside.

The other scrambled back, out of the way of falling branches. Jagged stone smashed into ground where he'd stood, broke apart in an explosion of debris and sound in blinding grays. The dragon roared its startled outrage at near demise by craven ruse, split the air with booming force as the other set came crashing down.

Through wing, scale and bone, stony limbs impaled both dragon and earth amidst a cacophony of wailing blues. His pained roars, a cloying white, were short and halfhearted, interrupted by the gurgle of filling lungs and violent spasms. Muscles parted, exposed to air, pulsed sickly sweet in ruddy movement.

Though the other was severely wounded, thoroughly pinned from tail to head, Stone knew he still posed a considerable threat. Stone took the time to circle wide, approached from his flank with tailed thrums, great caution and grave intent.

"Who told you where to find me?"

Bubbled laughter and bloody spittle gave rise to a fit of coughing, jagged crimson gone to black so foul it marred the taste.

"Now you find your tongue," the other said between ragged breaths. "It...a female...mountains..."

His words were muffled, interspersed with gulling whispers.

Mountains?

"What?" Stone moved in closer. "What female?"

The other's tail broke free its hold, through shattered tree limb and scaly flesh. It took Stone in full across the wing, a whoosh of pale shock that splintered bone and sent him sprawling. On his back, growling against the agony, Stone rolled over the broken wing and out of reach from snapping jaws.

Foolish curiosity had nearly killed him.

The other's tail was torn in half, swung wildly from side to side in a spray of waning warmth, as he fought in vain to wriggle free. Bile leaked in spasms from a wound at its throat, unable to ignite in its maw. Stone swung about with all his might, flared the ridges of his own tail and struck against the other's head. Horn and scales were sliced through, a bloody gob of skull pulled loose and both eyes reduced to whispered shreds. Stone moved in without pause, bit hard behind an ear. His jaws locked on, forced through the murk of hide and tendon to the muscle underneath. With vicious shakes, he finally caught hold of the bundled veins.

The other dragon bled out, as Stone collapsed.

* * *

Stone opened his eyes to home, to his mother's lair, with her looming over. He was on his back against a wall, right wing broken and torn. With a growing rumble of disapproval, her steady gaze seemed to burn through his chest, caused his heart to skip a beat at her seething regret.

"Look what you've done," she said, so overwrought she could barely speak, "wasted another life." She leaned in, close enough to feel her breath. "Is my son still in there?"

She searched his eyes, though for what he wasn't sure. Stone wanted to speak, to soothe her trembling, but knew she would take it as a sign of weakness. She looked down on him in disgust.

"All of it for naught," she fairly snarled. "You'll never fly, never hunt. You'll just be meal for another." Her eyes narrowed in decision. "May as well be mine."

Quick, without mercy, she bit deep into his throat...

"Stone!" It was Glim's voice in a striking gray and white, her touch upon his maw. "You were having a bad dream."

He sat up in confusion and tested his wing. Sore all throughout but thoroughly mended, even the membrane showed no trace of injury.

"What happened?"

He felt as if he'd slept for days. The ground beneath had gone to mud, a harsh swelter of smoky crimson. The flutter of breath from Glim's wings played out a rhythm of concern.

"You fell unconscious," she said, "and your wing began to heal. I'd always been told dragons had no magic of their own, that you were terrified of it."

Stone shook the fog from his brain and remembered the other dragon's words.

She said you'd be here. He turned toward the fey with a wary eye. Glim was the only female he knew.

"I have no magic," Stone said and got to his feet. "I've been eating the fruit Crier grows. Perhaps he's affected them in other ways."

Sense of the waiting meat grew his pangs of hunger to a ravenous ache. His stomach readied for a meal of its own accord.

"This one was told where to find me," Stone said, to gauge her reaction, "by a female."

Glim seemed puzzled by the notion. She looked up of a sudden with widened eyes.

"You think it was me?" she asked and crossed her arms. "And where would I have met another dragon? Why would I risk the only living tree I've seen in years?"

Stone grumbled at her rationale. He moved around the fallen dragon and tore into the remains at its flank, pulled aside scale and gristle with a claw. He bit away chunks of meat to the spray of sweet violets and maroons, swallowed them whole and went for more.

"Doesn't it make more sense she's another dragon?" Glim pressed. "An unhappy mate from your past? What else but another dragon could survive the conversation?"

"You survived ours," Stone noted, his maw dripping a cadence of ichor.

She cringed and backed away at the sight of his feeding, covered her mouth with a hand as if taken by sickness.

"You're assuming," she said, "this female knew you. You've been here in the forest long enough that she may have spotted you but was too small or weak to kill you on her own." Glim continued to look away as he fed, but the rhythm of her blood was steady as she spoke, her voice a smooth sequence of pale blues. "She could even be this one's mate."

"They would've attacked together."

"Maybe he attacked her," Glim offered, "and she bargained your location for her life."

"Then she is already dead," Stone stated plainly.

It did seem unlikely the fey could've told him. She wouldn't risk losing the great tree, and Stone doubted another dragon could be convinced to safeguard Crier.

Who then was this *she* the other spoke of?

Once he'd gorged enough to sate his middle a few long moments, he paused and considered. "I've never had a mate," he confided. "This tree is the only home I've known since I left my mother's lair. Before this, I spent my days in hiding or on the hunt."

"Food is scarce for everyone, but there are plenty of caves and old warrens all over." She hazarded a glance his way. "You couldn't find one that would suit you?"

"I didn't choose to burrow into the earth," he replied in a surly tone, "and cover myself with mud because I was picky about where to live." He pulled free the entrails to better reach at the underside. "I've gone moons at a time without a meal. It's been difficult to find an area that isn't already marked. No matter where I laid to rest, if I wasn't masked, something found me. If not a larger dragon," he said between bites, "then a pack of tuskers or an ursal, grousers or a pair of crawlers, displacers or howlers, stalkers or flayers." Blood and bits sang wildly as his ire grew. "Not once have I slept a full night in a new lair." He swallowed a hefty piece and moved on to the hind legs. "Not until I came here."

"That doesn't sound right," Glim said. "Even if you've never taken a lair, it's highly unlikely so many predators would've found you on their own."

What do feys know of dragons? he scoffed inwardly. *Especially one who's spent most of her life underground.*

"What exactly are you saying?"

"I know what it's like to be hunted," she said and met his gaze. "What I'm saying is, those creatures could've been driven toward you. I think someone or something has been using others to try to kill you, long before you ever arrived in this forest." She flew in closer, spoke in a solemn shade of inky blue. "Dragon or no, you're not like others I've met since...I was forced from my home. I see goodness in you. I would like to be your friend, but that isn't possible without trust."

Stone turned the unfamiliar word over in his mind. She hadn't said it with disrespect.

"Friend," he repeated. "I don't know what that is."

"Oh. Well, it's sort of..." Glim seemed surprised. "Do you have any siblings?"

Willowisp.

His heart sank. Though she'd never left his thoughts, he'd refused to wallow in the loss. Memory of their time together was a dichotomy of pain and joy. Try as he might, it was difficult to think of her without reliving those final moments.

"A sister."

"Let me guess," Glim said lightheartedly. "You ate her."

"Never would I have hurt her!" Stone glowered, and Glim backed away in fear. "I loved my sister!" He swallowed hard and looked away. "Willow and I shared a bond like no other."

"I—I'm sorry. I didn't mean—"

"Mother wanted me to eat her," Stone said, furious at the thought of her time and again trying to pit him against Willow. "I was clearly the stronger, but I saw in her worth beyond strength." The old pain of her loss filled his chest anew. "She was my other half. My better half."

Glim was there beside him, her touch an uncommon comfort of cool green in a sea of seething reds.

"Were you born from the same egg?" she asked.

"No, we weren't," he replied in a lighter tone, "though at times it seemed that way."

"Tell me. What happened?"

Stone recalled their flying high across the mountains of their home. After a few moments, he exhaled heavily and continued.

"When she thought we were ready, mother brought us to a hydra den. She killed the elder and left us to face its brood. There were six, all young but deadly." Stone's wings began to tremble with anger and remorse. "I was careless, allowed one to flank me as I chased another. Willow put herself in harm's way to protect me. When it was done, I was nearly unscathed, but she had suffered many wounds. One had struck the artery in her neck. There was nothing I could do but hold her until she died."

"I'm so sorry. That's terrible." Glim had difficulty speaking, her voice in sullen whites. "You must've loved her very much."

"When mother returned," he went on, shame burning his ears, "she thought I'd killed Willow along with the others in a frenzy. She was *proud.* It was the only time I'd ever seen my mother happy." Stone cleared his throat and blinked up at the swollen skies. "I never told her the truth."

Glim said, "The way you felt about your sister. That's what friendship is like. A friend is family of your own choosing, a bond forged through time and trial."

Stone shook his head, more to clear his cloying thoughts than in any answer.

"To have that once again..." He caught sight of Glim's smile, and it warmed him. "If that's truly what a friend is, then I should very much like to have one."

– 5 –

Rain fell anew all around him in the dark, embraced the world in a silver silhouette of lingered flashes and echoed rumbles. The wind carried with it the forest shape in its touch, the aged remnants of bole and branch in rhythm to the tumult, the battered and barren earth stretched out between trees and every rock laid bare to break the surface.

Stone paused at his meal for the third time that night. He took long steady breaths, mindful that his body needed to adjust and digest. He was anxious to be done with it and move the carcass far away. It would soon begin to attract others, if it hadn't already.

Glim perched in the great tree, upon one of the lower limbs wide enough for a dozen feys. A hollow in the trunk let her lay halfway within, protected somewhat from the storm. She sat cross-legged inside it, a second garment stretched up and over to block the rain.

Crier slept below, as if the storm provided comfort. The child's heart beat out a steady tempo, far more fast-paced than his own. Stone could feel it across his scales, a vibration that settled through and brought with it a sense of ease.

He wondered what he would do if this meal triggered a molt. His new scales already scraped at some points in the tunnel. If he were any larger, he'd have no choice but to move Crier out from the hidden chamber—or place his trust in Glim to care for the child. Stone shook his head at the thought. He wasn't quite ready for that yet and might never be.

Dragons were slow to trust for good reason.

Five winged figures took form in the distance, moving at a hurried pace and straight for the great tree. They were fey, like Glim, with long ears and longer hair. The sense of ursal wove about them like an earthen shroud, as if they wore animal flesh as garments. They carried weapons as well, of shaped wood and steel, enveloped in harsh whispers. It was a magic very different from the illusions within the tree, with the inky tingles of threat and deadly promise of danger. His mother had warned of such magic in stories about the Wardens, though none of those tales had included feys or their conclave.

"Glim," Stone called, so his voice carried through the storm. He moved quickly to stand in front of the tunnel entrance and considered his options. "Feys are headed this way. All five are male and have weapons of magic."

She left her hollow by wing and fluttered in air beside him, followed his gaze out into the trees.

"Hunting parties don't go above ground," she said, her words in pale echoes of unrestrained fear. "It's too dangerous. They have to be conclave." Her pained look grew apologetic. "If they're scouts or trackers, they must have followed me here. I can lead them away. If they're agents..."

Glim shook her head in distress.

"I'm so sorry," she said.

Stone had never faced magic as a weapon, knew only

what his mother had told him. Though he was frightened at the prospect, he'd long ago learned there was little in this world to be unafraid of. All life was prey, at one time or another. Every breath was hard won, fought for and deserved by the strong. Fear was good. It had kept him healthy, cautious and aware, and ultimately out of the mouths of better prey.

They might not be here for her, Stone considered. *If she tries to lead them away, she'll only make them aware of her presence.*

"Could they have heard the battle?" he asked, sensed them stalk closer with every breath.

"It doesn't matter why they're here," she said. There was defeat in her tone, the sullen gray of despair. "You have to take Crier and leave. There's no other way. I'll do what I can to draw them off."

Glim then did the strangest thing. She flew in close, pressed the warmth of her lips to a soft fold above his eye and disappeared into the nighttime shadows.

Stone's mind began to work.

Could the unknown female that had sent a dragon against him be involved? Could she be in league with the same feys that wanted Glim? Or did this conclave merely track Glim here? Or did Glim lead them here in exchange for her life and freedom?

He discarded the notions with a firm shake of his head. Time was running short, if he wanted to get down to Crier and be away with the child. The feys would soon be close enough to use their weapons. If he chose to trust Glim, to be her friend, he couldn't let her risk be for nothing. The Warden's survival was more important than the both of them.

*But if she is a friend...*Stone growled in frustration. *Never would I have let Willow face such a danger alone.*

Glim's sense reappeared within quick, ashen pulses,

determined trills of fevered steps moving in and out of shadow. Though deathly afraid, she ran headlong into peril. Reckless cries drew their attention. Nimble feet dodged their attacks. The magicked arrows they loosed lit the forest in passing. Bright whistling and forked spark, like shards of charged storm, the wooden missiles tore through stony branch and crackled the earth with every strike.

If they hadn't known the great tree was alive before entering the forest, regardless of why they'd come, they certainly knew it now. The only choices left to Stone were to take Crier and flee the forest or kill these agents of the conclave. Their deaths would afford him more time, to leave Glim and the child safely hidden while he looked for a new lair.

What if this conclave already knew of the tree? Glim seemed sure there was nothing Stone could do to stop them. What did she know that he didn't? How could a handful of feys stand a chance against him? But if they did know, wouldn't they have sent more than five to face him? They were either foolishly confident or unaware of his presence.

That could give him some advantage.

Stone eyed the great tree, fought down the urge to go for Crier. He'd decided to help his friend. Once the agents had been dealt with, he could take the child and Glim with him in search of a new lair. Their home had been discovered. It was no longer safe to stay, no matter the outcome.

He pushed off from the muddied earth and took wing in a single beat. Stone kept to the dark, stayed out of the moonlight and was careful to put trees between him and the other feys as he moved. Unlike them, he didn't need to see to know exactly where they were. Still, he had to be cautious. These agents wielded lethal magic, and none of them were afraid to use it. He'd need to rely on cunning and guile to survive the fight. Brute force was rarely the best first option.

He imagined Glim was strongest at night, when the shadows were most abundant, but she had chosen her physical form to lure the five away. She began to veer left, just out of range of their weapons. The three in front drew sharpened blades that sang with enchantment and glowed bright in a halo all about them. The remaining two continued to take aim with bow and fired slivers of whispered light. Glim wove between trees to avoid being hit. The shafts struck all around her and crackled like lightning, before sizzling out into smoke.

Why aren't they flying after her?

Glim had deftly avoided getting too close but was nearly taken by more than one arrow in her attempt to draw them off. Except the agents didn't give chase. They kept right on for the great tree.

Did they know about Crier? Had Glim or this other female told them? Even if the agents didn't know about the child, they surely sensed the tree had come back to life. What else could do such a thing besides a Warden?

Stone stopped and looked back, no longer sure he was making the right decision.

Glim had stopped as well and turned back toward the five. She disappeared into shadow and moments later reappeared among them, sent one archer sprawling with a kick. Though Stone could see nothing in her hands, he could sense the shadow blades she firmly held and used to block incoming strikes of steel and bow. One began conjuring spheres of light to brighten the forest, while another called fire to his sword and offhand.

There was no longer any doubt of her allegiance, but Stone began to wonder if she'd ever taken a life. Not an animal on the hunt, but another sentient being. Deep down, she must have known what had to be done, but if she was afraid to cross that line, to spill the blood of her own people, she was putting her life at greater risk.

Any hesitation could mean her end.

A sudden flutter in his stomach, Stone was no longer merely interested to see how far she'd go, whether she'd do what needed to be done to protect Crier. No, he felt a pang of worry for her safety. Eyes narrowed and breath heated, he thrust forward to close the distance. His first instinct was to kill from afar, either smash the treetops far above and let death rain down upon them or set them all afire with his breath. Stone paused and cursed. Both tacks put Glim in danger.

The five wove magic through the air in time to their attacks, sent Glim reeling out of range to avoid being struck. She was outnumbered and outmagicked, but she used the very darkness as a weapon, disappearing into it and striking from behind. Unfortunately, that darkness was slipping away, as more spheres of light emerged and hung suspended in the air. Magic flared around each agent like a shell of azure song when slashed by her blades, yet their weapons had no trouble reaching her. Glim had cuts on both arms and along her side before Stone could even move to engage.

Stone roared out a challenge, foregoing surprise, and circled the group. He hoped to take their attention off Glim, to give her time for a decisive strike or escape.

"No!" she screamed up at him. "I told you to go!"

Glim disappeared and emerged behind the one with a fiery sword, kicked out his left leg and knocked the blade aside for an offhand strike. A second swung at her thigh. His weapon billowed with green mist that eroded all it touched into pocks and smoking ruin. She disappeared in time to avoid it, but the one barking orders must have anticipated her reaction. He caught Glim off guard as she stepped from shadow, landed a blow across her temple with the pommel of his sword. Frost and ice crystal ran the length of his blade, left her skin crackling with cold where it had touched. Glim stumbled and fell onto her back. The second quickly closed in and leveled kicks at her head to keep her down.

"Keep firing on the dragon," the lead fey told the two with bows. "It's just a young male. It won't attack."

He pulled a corded length from his belt, similar to Glim's garment, the slick blues of spider silk. He kicked her in the side, knelt down by her chest, then struck her hard across the jaw. She slumped back, unconscious. He began to bind her arms and legs at the outer joints, as a multitude of arrows raced upward through the storm.

Stone was afraid what they had planned for her. By her own account, they wanted her dead. So why not just kill her here?

Unless they wanted to bring her home, he thought, *to hold her captive. Or worse. And what did the one mean I was* just *a young male, that I wouldn't attack?*

They must have dealt with dragons in the past. Did their magic protect against breath? Could he risk getting close enough to be struck by those blades? More arrows lit the night and whistled past, dangerously close to his wings. The third fey reached down to pull Glim over a shoulder. All five then resumed their march for the great tree.

Stone growled out a sigh.

There was no ruse or clever attack that wouldn't put Glim in harm's way. He dove down toward the forest floor and circled through the trees, around to their flank. He swooped in behind them and breathed a short stream of fire on the right side, far enough away to avoid Glim but still bathe one of the archers in flame. Magic flared around the fey and wavered as he leapt aside. A stronger blast might have torn through.

So they are protected by magic, Stone confirmed, *but that magic has its limits.*

He flew straight up, wove around trees to block the barrage of arrows.

"I thought it wouldn't attack!" the one carrying Glim said angrily.

Stone sensed him set her down and begin to chant in a strange language, one that coalesced into glowing whispers. He moved both hands in a growing melody of wide arcs that conjured purple flame. A spell? The others spread out. Stone sensed in them little fear and realized they were trying to make it difficult for him to use his breath on more than one at a time. The two with bows were unrelenting, could not have carried with them so many arrows. If those too were born of magic, rather than fashioned, there would be no end to their assault.

"There's something off about this one," the lead fey said. "Take it alive, if you can. The Grand Magister can never have too many pets."

Stone halted in air, allowed himself to fall and turn about, then soared straight down. On the other side of a large tree, the five couldn't see his descent. He pulled up at the last, gripped the tree with a claw to slow his turn and swung around just behind them. He landed with the other claw protectively covering Glim and lashed out with his tail in a wide circle a few scale lengths above the ground.

Two were struck full on and went flying off into the night. The floating spheres of muffled light winked out of existence, threw the forest into darkness but for the glare of magic blades. The one nearest Stone finished his spell and set loose the ball of fiery violet he'd conjured. It shot up toward Stone's neck like a tiny sun. Though it looked small, the heat of its passing was more intense than any dragonfire. Stone dodged the brunt of its mystic flames, but the scales of his right shoulder had been scorched into curled char.

He brought bile to his throat in a steady clenching of stomach muscles. A single click of his back teeth, and a spark set it all alight. Stone loosed the stream straight down onto the fey caster. It tore past his magic shield and burned straight through to the bone. He barely voiced a scream before his body blackened and fell apart into bloody cinders and ashen wing.

The remaining archer quickly ducked behind a tree and began to fire from cover. One ripped through Stone's right wing as if it were nothing at all, tore and burned away at the membrane as it passed. He closed his wings on instinct to protect them, but the damage had been done. Pain shot down his backside with every pulsing of his heart. Two more shafts struck the scales of his shoulder and chest, before Stone spat back a stream of fire. The fey slipped behind the tree to avoid the flames, but Stone was sure he'd sensed a bit lick past the magic barrier and catch on hardened garment.

The lead fey climbed to his feet and called magical ice to his blade. It burned with a blue fire and dripped icicles upon the muddied ground. He leapt forward, stabbed at Stone's left foreclaw and dodged aside for more attacks. Glim was still safe, shielded beneath the other claw. By the flutter of wing against his palm, he could sense her begin to stir.

Though Stone was quick to react, he still suffered a cut across two knuckles and then another to his palm as he pulled away from the attack. The blade had parted his scales. Its magic hissed and crackled with painful ice at the edges. It felt as if the frost began to spread, numbing his claw from within. He tried to crush the lead fey, who rolled aside and out of reach, but only managed to gouge deep tracks into the earth.

"What are you?" the fey asked, as if he was no longer sure what he faced.

"Just a young dragon," Stone growled out his reply in a mock tone.

He swung his tail at the archer, who'd thought Stone distracted. About to fire, the fey was caught by surprise and a swift strike. He tried to slip behind the tree again, but Stone's tail went clean through. It shattered bole and fey alike, sent the archer careening end over end like a broken child.

"A dragon would have fled," the lead fey said with a grimace, his fear buried beneath contempt. He tightened his grip, readying to strike. "You are something else."

Stone breathed fire in a wide arc at the ground in front. He didn't want to risk another hit from that icy blade and sensed one of the first he'd attacked flying back toward them.

While the lead fey guarded his eyes from the flames, Stone closed his claw about Glim with care and took wing. He carried her back to the great tree, shielded her from magic and storm with his body. The flight pained his wings with every beat, but he endured for her sake—for all their sakes. He put her down at the base of the tree, sliced through her bonds with a talon and went to retrieve Crier. The child Warden had slept through the entire ordeal.

Stone took him up, went back out for Glim and flew them both north out of the forest.

– 6 –

They flew for hours before sunrise peaked over the horizon, where the Wall forever beckoned him onward. It was like no other mountain, if it could be called one at all. Rather than a squat base of eroded rock that led up to craggy peaks, it stood as a testament to Warden magic and a reminder of why they'd been hunted to extinction. They'd used their power to crack open the earth, reached down to its core and forced up one end. The breach was so high not even a dragon could surmount it, if one could survive the eternal storm at its summit. An unnatural torrent of violet black and bright flash that never faded, the chaotic clouds were thought to be the result of magic gone awry.

He'd been told no dragon would dare go there, not for fear of the tempest or its wild magic but for the mass of shadwens in its dark. The Wall ran with the rising sun, should have brightened with its touch but was said to host a shadow at its feet no sunlight could prevail. It stretched for hours by wing and was home to an untold number of terrible creatures of darkness and smoke. Ferocious and insubstantial, able to change shape at will, nothing could harm a shadwen but the light of day.

Stone didn't know how much of what he'd been told was fanciful story, but his mother had never ventured beyond the vale. A stretch of hilly wasteland between two ranges, it was three days from the Wall. They'd passed the first mountain of the eastern range an hour back. His wing had healed along the way but caused trouble at the start. He'd been forced to veer wide around claimed lairs but sensed fewer and fewer dragons the closer they drew north.

As much as the stories had frightened him, he found allure in the notion of a place without other dragons.

Stone forced his attention from the Wall, from the reverie of a life without danger. He wanted to put as much distance between themselves and the conclave as he could, but they needed to find shelter as soon as possible. Flying with Crier and Glim was reckless and dangerous for all three. Any encounter with them in hand would only end in disaster.

She had woken twice but still suffered from wounds to her head and side. Without the fruit Crier caused to grow, he knew of no other way but time to help her heal. While awake, she'd told him the conclave had no magical means of transport. Trackers could try to find them, but their agents would be on foot. Stone's instincts told him no distance was too great.

He eyed The Wall and chuckled.

Would they follow into the shadow? he wondered and recalled the lead fey. *I can't imagine a fitter end than a dozen shadwens at your flesh.*

Though his wing had healed from the magic arrow, his claw had been much slower to mend. He'd been right not to press the attack. Another slash from that icy blade might have meant all their lives. He held both claws to his chest to shield them from the wind. Crier had woken and cried as they left the forest, but the airstream and rhythmic flight had seemed to lull him once the storm had ceased.

Stone spotted a small cave, sensed no other life and risked setting down. He thumped his tail a quick rhythm, felt nothing in the echoed images and called bile to this throat. He let it loose in a billowing cacophony of fire, a familiar song that scorched the walls and ate away any impurity. Abandoned lairs, especially ones with water, were notorious for causing sickness.

With great care, he opened his left claw and let Glim slip down to her feet. He gave her a gentle nudge, held her upright until she woke. Once she was fully aware, he opened his other claw and offered her Crier.

"Keep watch," he said.

Glim took the child in both hands beneath the arms, with such a delicate touch and affection she might as well have been handling treasure. She pulled him in and held the baby in the crook of her left arm, tightened the blanket about him and touched lips to his forehead.

"Thank you," she said to Stone. He could feel in the flushed glimmer of her tone that she was keenly aware of the trust he'd place in her. "Have we gone far enough?"

"For now," he said and looked out over the lower hills to the west. It wouldn't be long before the rains turned to snow. "This cave will keep you hidden while I search for a better lair. I've marked it with my breath. Nothing but another dragon will come near until dark."

She kept Crier's head pressed firmly to her chest and covered his other ear with her hand as he'd spoke. Was his voice not already quiet enough?

"We should stay together," she said.

"If I find something worth claiming," Stone explained, "I'll have to fight for it. Any shelter worth having will be taken."

Glim's forehead creased, and her sense blossomed with worry.

"Why not stay here until morning, start fresh again tomorrow?" She gave his wounded claw a critical look. "You should at least wait until you're healed."

Stone tested its strength with a clenched fist and found the pain acceptable. His flesh had already closed, and the scales were nearly mended. He guessed it had taken this long for Crier's magic to heal him because the wound had been inflicted by an enchanted weapon.

"It's healed enough." He considered her part in the fight, had been struck by an idea. "During the fight," he said and tried to speak even more quietly when Crier began to stir, "I saw you use the shadows to attack. You can hide within them if you choose. Could you take Crier with you?"

A single shake of her head, and her flesh seemed to pulse with the pale crimson of sadness and prickled tone of shame.

"My mother never had a chance to teach me." She swallowed and added, "I—I wouldn't leave him, though. To save myself. No matter what happens. I'd never do that."

Stone hadn't even thought it a possibility.

Why mention it at all? he wondered. *I neither showed nor expressed doubt.* He could sense the turmoil within her, the raucous scent of emotion. *Ahh. She struggles with her past.*

He knew all too well the pain of a haunted memory and thought it best to let her be. Wings spread and legs tensed, he readied for flight.

"Wait," Glim said before he could leave. "If there is someone or something else besides the coven tracking you, trying to kill you, then we don't just need a safe place. The forest was safe. What we need is a place to hide, someplace underground."

Stone considered her reasoning. Though he disliked being unable to see the sky at any moment, their need to remain hidden was undeniable. He'd suffered far worse discomforts in his lifetime.

He gave a nod and took wing.

He climbed up into the cold and gray mist beneath the clouds, as high as he could and still sense the ground below. If anything had followed them, was still keeping watch, he wanted to find and kill it slowly. The idea that something had been stalking him, trying to kill him from afar, either toying with or torturing him with all the relentless attacks, was infuriating.

What sort of creature would that be, if not another dragon? One most likely older and far larger.

It was the only explanation he could fathom. Nothing else would've been able to command a dragon to attack him. How long had this been happening to him? He'd been harrowed and harassed since leaving his mother's lair, or at least it seemed so in retrospect. At the time, he merely thought the world a dangerous place for one so small. They'd certainly never been attacked while he lived with his mother. He'd attributed that to her size and age. An idea struck him, a terrible notion.

What if all these attacks have been tests? he fairly growled. *What if the mysterious female plaguing my every step has been mother?*

She'd never seemed to truly care for him, but she'd always kept him safe. Maybe it wasn't her intention to kill him but to make him stronger, toughen him with one ordeal after another. It reminded him of the hydra den and loss of his sister. Willowisp, the only happiness he'd ever known, was forever gone because of such a test. It had all begun to make sense, to fall into place.

Stone was suddenly overcome with the desire to claw

out his mother's heart.

He shook his head to clear the anger from clouding sense and judgement, let the burning hatred fall away from his chest. He had a task to see through, lives that depended on him. Whether it was his mother or not made no difference now. He'd seen nothing from this vantage, dragon or otherwise.

What he needed was a delver warren, one close to a mountain or large hill that could mask an entrance. He flew to the nearest crag, a short distance by wing, and descended to its bottom. In a slow circuit about the base, he began searching for sense of life. His attention divided between the rushing echoes above and below, he turned over rocks and thumped the earth with both claws in steady intervals. The practiced pace formed a series of seamless images in his mind, the tawny pitch of earthen layers, the vacant murmurs of fallen tunnel, the acerbic twinge and saline chill of clay and rock.

Stone came to a sliding halt at the muted spread of resounding air. Rapid thumps of his tail began to fashion a clearer picture, but the cavern was already at the very edge of his sense. He couldn't discern all its features or even gauge how deep it went.

He followed the vibrations to their closest point in the mountain and loosed his breath upon the surface. Once the rock softened, he clawed away molten chunks at a downward angle. On more than one occasion, he'd been forced to hide this way. By creating an overhang of shaped slag, he concealed the burrow well enough that any creature flying by would have needed more than a cursory look to find him. This time he wasn't making a hole to hide in.

Stone continued the long process of tunneling into the mountain and down toward the cavern. It took hours of patience and relentless perseverance, but he broke through to the delver warren. A chiming gust brushed past, the faded blue of distant currents. There must have been another way to the surface far off in the distance.

The cavern was truly massive, a naturally occurring hollow deep underground. Light radiated out from veins in the rock, thick bands of heady gold in a semblance of sun. At some point, a delver must have made it a home. The walls and floor had ridges scored into them in spots, sign of the long claws one had used to expand its warren. Stone searched the entire area and found nothing but two more tunnels leading north and west. Both gradually dropped in depth and branched out to more tunnels.

Careful not to damage the main cavern, he collapsed both and closed them off. He returned to what was now the only entrance and cleared away any debris left over from his tunneling. He carried larger rocks away and melted what was left. It took more time and care to fly over the opening, to further shape it and ensure it looked natural. Once he was satisfied, Stone began to feel an anxious flurry in his middle.

What he had found wasn't ideal by any stretch of the imagination, but it was enough for the time being. He'd been away for too long. Stone took to the air and hurried back to Glim and Crier.

* * *

That winter was difficult.

They hadn't brought Crier's egg, so Stone fashioned a new one from rock. He also went into a molt shortly after arriving, which left him weak and uneasy while his new scales hardened. They decided it was best if Stone stayed hidden within the cavern. While that meant it was harder for the conclave to track them, or for his mother to find and torment him any further, it also meant he couldn't hunt.

They relied on what Crier caused to grow and what Glim brought back from her trips foraging in the Hollow, the subterranean world where her people had built their new home. Her ability to travel through shadow, to pass from one to another a wingspan away, made it easy for her to traverse the long distance during the night. While she promised to stay away from the main city, where the conclave was strongest, Stone didn't like that she risked being caught for meager food and trinkets.

She brought back meat for him, precious little but enough to remind him what he was, and many things for Crier they could not otherwise provide: clothes, shoes, blankets, bedding, a pillow, toys, books and even treats.

By spring, the cavern was half filled with new life, as if Crier's touch reached slowly but inexorably outward. Stone wondered how far that reach might go. Already they'd had to deal with a flock of redwings, a pair of cutters from a distant colony and a return of the cavern's delver. While Stone enjoyed the meals, he would rather not worry that at any moment their growing paradise would attract more danger.

The ground around Crier's stone egg had become rich soil, with a pungent, thick layer of lush grass and budding flora. Where the flowers and vines grew dense, they seemed to commingle into roots, as if the magic that brought them life sought to join them into trees. Stone mused that the child missed their once forest home and yearned to forge them another.

While no sunlight reached down the tunnel and into the cavern, the unusual mineral that spread the length of its walls provided ample glow. The webwork of crystal bands ranged between a ruddy yellow in full bloom and a muted pale of nighttime quiet, and on rare occasion pitched to a brilliant silver. It protruded in rippled bulbs where the rock was densest and was even warm to the touch at peak brightness. When moss began to appear across the walls, the crystal radiance beneath pushed through like a softened sunfall. Watching that glow grow and fade throughout the day reminded Stone of the outside world.

All that was missing were the stars.

Since Crier was hatched so close to winter, with the next one that came Glim brought him a gift to celebrate his first year of birth. She claimed to know the exact day she was born, but Stone found the entire notion to be ridiculous. It was then he asked her what a year was and learned his mother had lied. She'd told him dragons had killed the Wardens and set fire to the forests well over a thousand turns ago. In truth, it had been little more than ten.

He then often wondered what other of her stories had been lies, to reason out her motives or understand her unmasked hatred for him and Willow. According to Glim, there was no bond stronger than the love of a mother for her children.

Clearly they had led different lives.

Glim's gesture led to a tradition, where each of them received a gift in celebration of their birth. Stone had been hatched in winter, or so he'd been told, while Glim had been born on the summer solstice. It was a day when the sun shone brighter and longer than any other, and she'd been named in honor of its brilliance.

By Crier's second birthday, he'd sprouted hair on top and had been walking for some time in a wobbly but enthusiastic manner. Glim's gift for him was a wooden ball she'd fashioned from one of the now many trees that inhabited the cavern. It was bigger than his tiny palm, but he loved to pick it up with both hands and throw it with an excited laugh. It would bounce and roll away through the tall grass, and Crier would chase after with a happy squeal.

It was during one of these times of play that Stone sensed something come alive beneath Crier's touch. The child had placed a hand against a tree, and the creature stepped from its bark. It was as if it had been stuck there all along, and Crier had set it free. In alarm, Stone moved to intervene, but Glim was already there. She picked the child up and turned away, used her body as a shield.

The creature didn't appear to be aggressive though or seem to mean any harm. It just stood there, waiting, no taller than her knee.

"It looks like a living splinter," Stone noted.

"Or a small tree," Glim said once she'd hazarded a glance. "A treeling?"

It stood on moving roots no longer than a scale, two in front and back and with questionable balance. A pair of arms like fragile branches sprouted out from its twiggy body, leafless but equally mobile. Its lidless eyes were knots and its mouth a gaping bulge. The whole of its being whispered magic in a way much like their forest.

It dawned on Stone then just how accustomed he'd grown to the constant thrum and echoes of Crier's touch. The child's magic was all around them, every moment of every day, growing higher and spreading wider in a crowd of hushed murmurs.

Whether by Crier's bidding or not, the treeling began to shamble off. It gathered the wooden ball into both its leafless hands and returned. Glim set Crier down, and the treeling offered him the ball. He took it up and threw it again with a shout of laughter. The treeling went chasing after without complaint.

Though it didn't speak a language either Stone or Glim could discern, it did seem to communicate with voiced creaks and stiff body movements. It got around rather quickly on its four spindly legs but couldn't lift much with the branches at its sides.

Crier called the creature Notch.

Over time, the treeling blossomed on top with tiny boughs, thickened and grew leaves, though never quite looked a proper tree. The two would talk and play for hours, once Crier had finished all his chores.

The menial tasks had been Glim's idea, were meant to instill discipline and respect. She insisted on teaching him all manner of things, to which Stone was grateful for the time alone. While he enjoyed his time with Crier, the games of chase, of hide and seek, their simple talks and daytime naps, he also longed to be in air. The draw of rushing wind called out to him from above, whistled in luring blues down the tunnel entrance.

The best Stone could manage were waking dreams in quiet solitude, where his musings often led to a single, painful conclusion: Dragons were never meant to live underground. His sacrifice, his willingness to endure in hiding for Crier's safety, stood as a testament for how much he had grown to care for the child.

By five years, Crier had learned to read and write, to fight with staff and sword, could climb the tallest tree and began to practice Warden magic. Oddly enough, it was Stone who helped direct him. Glim had tried, offered what she knew of fey mages and shadow walking, but the dragon seemed to have an innate grasp of Warden spellwork. He was adept at reading cues, used his perfect sense to gauge and guide the child's progress. Together, they explored the budding limits of Crier's abilities, until the tingled whispers of his magic were as comforting as his touch.

"I can hear them," Crier said with widened eyes, an ear pressed to Stone's belly.

"If you mean the whines and gurgles," Stone said and

looked down with a doubting eye, "then perhaps you could return to the task at hand."

The little Warden had been trying to sprout new life in barren earth, when he'd been distracted by a voice.

"Not those!" he said and laughed, rapped knuckles against a scale as if expecting a reply. "Something else."

Crier heard voices in everything around him, spoke with nature in all its aspects. From trees to earth, rocks to flowing stream, even the very air, he drew knowledge from their touch and claimed to hear them whisper. He may not have had the senses of a dragon, but there were moments when it seemed he was part of another world.

By the time he was eight, he could not only conjure treelings and send them back to the trees that spawned them, he could manifest creatures from other elements as well. Temporary companions, of them all, only Notch remained. The treeling grew alongside and even started to surpass him.

Stone looked at the home they had built, far greater than any lair he could have imagined. The forest stood three times his height and continued on. Its trees bore a multitude of fruits and nuts, always seemed to be in bloom and breathed life into the cavern. Even the walls were covered in an emerald melody of growth, from a springy layer of azure moss to the lilting scrape of wild vines. The lambent cry of colored flowers sprang up from all around, within the rustle of tall grass, between the flare of underbrush and interspersed among the glow of new roots reaching outward.

Stone rested on his back, Crier sprawled across his belly, when both of them caught sense of another dragon far above. Stone was up in an instant and headed for the tunnel entrance. Crier had hung on, climbed scales up and over to settle in between two spine ridges. Notch bounded after, but there was no time to secure the treeling.

The other dragon had sensed them too.

There wasn't enough room to fly within the tunnel. Stone used both claw and wing to pull himself forward as he ran, scrambled to reach the outcrop and broke free into the air. He still had the advantage. The other hadn't sensed the cavern entrance yet and was still circling the mountain. Stone was nearly to the winter clouds, before the other male caught sense and gave chase.

While the fruit Crier caused to grow allowed Stone to heal with incredible speed, it hadn't offered him the same level of sustenance needed to fuel a molt. It had staved off the pain of hunger all these years, but dragons needed meat to grow. The few encounters and lack of hunting had left him not much bigger than when they first entered the cavern.

Cloud cover wouldn't hide them, but Stone hoped to use the greater height to dive down into the other. If he could strike at the neck or just behind a wing, the fight would be over without a single bite or claw strike.

A gout of flame erupted from below, a billow of harsh glow that expanded out like the morning rise of summer sun. It set the winds alight in caustic eddies of ashen motes.

"He seems angry," Crier called out over the rush of air, struggled to look below and maintain his grip.

The other male had long tail spikes, double spades along the spine and overlapping scales like an outcry of violet shimmer. Four wide horns spiraled outward from above and below its ears. One was cracked to a blunted half, with a split down its middle. Despite a small tear in its right wing, it gained speed and began to climb with a powerful thrust.

"Be careful," Stone warned.

They'd flown together in the cavern, but outside was

a different matter. Unexpected wind and strong currents could unseat him if he wasn't wary. Stone was smaller by a third, planned to use Crier's magic to frighten the other dragon. The boy was in no real danger, so long as he—

"I'll go talk to him," Crier said and leapt off.

"Wait!" Stone whirled about in wild shock, saw him soaring downward. "Crier, no!"

He followed with all haste, wings tucked to gather speed. The twisting sense of two airlings emerged on either side of Crier, guided his fall toward the other dragon and slowed him to a safe descent. He landed on the male's neck, even though it had sensed his approach and tried to evade. At a safe spot behind the ears, the boy appeared to be having a one-sided conversation. The dragon writhed and spun madly to throw him off.

Stone was nearly upon them, when he heard the echoed whispers of magic. The other dragon's eyes began to droop and close, as if it had fallen asleep in air. The two began to plummet in a lazy spiral toward the ground. Stone caught hold by the outer bones of both wings and set wide his own. His claws had plunged through, tore apart the membrane and shattered the fragile bones. It was all he could do to keep from joining the impending impact.

Crier leapt onto Stone's leg and began to climb back up. Airlings lent a hand, their eyes a flash of sapphire within the humanoid whirl of air. Stone let the dragon fall. It rolled into a heap, severely damaged but alive. He landed hard beside it and glared over a shoulder.

"Don't do that again," he warned the child. "Ever."

"I wanted to talk to him," Crier said in his defense and climbed down for a closer look, "but he wouldn't see reason."

Stone circled the sleeping dragon to its neck.

"You could've been injured," he said, upset with the

young Warden but losing all focus to the prospect of a proper meal. "Or worse."

"I knew you wouldn't let me get hurt." Crier put a hand to its chest, as if feeling for a heartbeat. "Just like I'd never let anyone hurt you."

Stone looked to his young friend with concern, didn't want him to see what came next.

"You know what I have to do."

Crier raised his eyes and gave a weak smile.

"I know," he said and looked away. "I know."

The boy walked off a short distance and knelt over the barren earth. He called magic to his hand, a small pyre of emerald fire. Crier busied himself with practice to give his friend some time alone.

Stone began to feed.

– 7 –

Three more winters went by in quiet solitude within the cavern, without sense of another dragon or incident but a fall. Crier had lost his footing while leaping from bough to branch in a reckless race against an airling. It had reacted quickly enough to catch him before striking the frozen ground but not in time to prevent fracturing his left arm on a passing tree limb.

It was during the painful days that followed when they learned the fruit's healing properties only affected Stone. Glim had tested it as well, with a nick of her shadow blade against a palm. For whatever reason, the fruit's magic seemed only to work on dragons.

Stone had encouraged Crier to use the injury as an opportunity, to mend the break on his own and push the limits of his magic. For long hours at a time, they sat together in the forest and worked at nothing else. Stone kept Crier warm by heating a ring of rocks with a stream of controlled flame, the way he had when his friend was just a baby.

Crier was nearly a man now, according to Glim. A few more years and he would cease to grow. It was strange to Stone that no matter how much the boy ate, he would never molt and shed his skin. Even Glim had molted at least once, though by her description it was more a hibernation in crystal. Apparently, feys weren't born with their wings.

Stone looked over at him with a sense of pride at how far he'd come. Crier had thick tufts of brown hair on top cut short by a dagger, bright eyes the lively hue of turned soil, peppered stubble upon his cheek and an expression of determined focus. Glim had said he was handsome for a human but that looks shouldn't matter. He had a kind heart and a quick wit. Everything else was just for show, like a set of fancy clothes.

"I can't do it," Crier said. He'd let out a deep breath he'd been holding, as if trapping air in his lungs might help him concentrate. "It's useless."

"Even if you're unsuccessful," Stone said, "your arm will still heal on its own. You have nothing to lose in the trying but time." He breathed heat into another stone when he sensed Crier begin to shiver. A thought came to him then. "Have you tried heat?"

"I've sent magic into the break," Crier replied, "but it only makes it hurt. I've tried drawing magic away from the area, picturing it in my mind, forcing the image to mend. Nothing seems to work!"

"When you revitalize soil, you call fire to your hand."

"It's not really fire," he said. "It's my magic, my inner essence interacting with the world around me. It changes color depending on what I interact with, what I'm doing, but it doesn't generate heat."

"But it could," Stone surmised, "if you use your mind to guide the interaction, alter it from within rather than letting it happen on its own."

"But I don't know how to do that!" Crier sat back on his legs hard and winced when the motion jerked his injured arm. He let out a sigh of frustration. "That's not how magic works."

Stone chuckled.

"You don't know how magic works any more than I do. That's why we're here," he said and warmed another rock, "practicing, exploring, learning what you can and cannot do. Tell me, what is red to you?"

"Like peonies?" Crier asked. "Blood, I suppose. Parts of the sunset, when it touches over the mountain."

Stone let the last go by unnoticed. Crier was not to leave the cavern on his own but often snuck up the tunnel for a peek at the outside world.

"For you," Stone said, "it's just a color, but it can be so much more. Red is the wild edge of fire striving to break free. It's the fervor of coursing blood, the blinding embrace of a summer sun. It's more than what you can see with your eyes. It's a feeling, an emotion, like an angry autumn blossoming inside. You can call up that red within you, drape it around your heart, let it embrace and envelop your inner essence."

Crier held out a palm and closed his eyes. Emerald fire bloomed to life in an exhalation of whispers. It licked along his flesh, wavered flickers from jade to pale. The hushed bits of winter glow carried up to a gentle flurry, began to turn end over end then darkened to pale rose. Further the fires went, into a swirl of spreading crimson, the deep red of a howling slash, the mired cry of a bloody tumult. Heat spread from it in waves, obscured his hand in diffuse shimmer.

"Good," Stone said, "but temper it with wind, a cool and soothing breeze. Draw out the healing warmth, and keep the fire at bay." The flames turned a crisp azure, a frozen storm within the blue. "Not too far off, now. Keep it just out of reach, before the heat becomes a burn."

The magic softened to sky blue, a lyric blossom of

whispers and guarded warmth. Crier opened his eyes, and its glinting was mirrored in them. He touched the flame to his injury. It lit veins beneath his flesh in a web of flowing, brilliant blue. Crier breathed a sigh of relief, one that grew into a smile.

"It worked," he said and tested his arm. "It's healed." He looked up at Stone in wonder. "How did you know to do that?"

"I—I didn't," Stone replied, taken aback for a short moment. "I just imagined what it must feel like, to have magic like yours. It was nothing."

"Nothing?" Crier climbed to his feet. "Nothing!" He laughed and embraced Stone at the maw. "You were brilliant!" He pulled back and looked down at his arm in amazement. "I have to show Glim."

He ran off toward the tree house, though it was more apt to call it a tree hole. One of the larger grandwoods once had a split above its base. When Glim described what the great tree had looked like, Crier set out to create one of his own. He used magic to further shape the recess into an opening, pushed deep into the trunk and widened it into a room. There was a bed of cloth and pillows inside, with a woven blanket for warmth, and his old stone egg which he now used to store books.

Crier had offered to share the tree with Glim, but she politely declined, stating it was improper. The objection was no doubt related to her issues with modesty. She'd often gone on about it when Crier had refused to wear clothing as a child. She'd insisted, however, and the boy still wore layers of leather and spider silk garment as a result.

Glim, on the other hand, preferred to slumber in the wide branches. She'd fashioned covers of netted branch and interwoven leaves, secured them to either side as makeshift walls. It didn't fool his dragon sense, but he wasn't sure if it was meant to. He'd heard her explain the need of privacy to Crier before, but as often was the case when she took that tone of voice, Stone had chosen to close his eyes and rest rather than listen.

Days later, as Crier practiced, he looked over and seemed about to speak. Stone didn't need to open an eye. The rumination and need to share it was like a palpable force, an anxious murmur on the verge of voice and a pensive tapping upon his knee.

"What is it?" Stone asked, still on the very edge of daytime dream.

"The egg," he replied. A question? At least he stopped tapping. "The one you found me in, the one Wardens had made and enchanted."

Stone let loose a sigh that rustled fallen leaves into a roll. They'd had this discussion before.

"I know," Crier said. "You think it's too soon. But I've learned everything I can from what's here. I need that egg for study. If Wardens constructed it, I can use it to learn more about them, to be a better Warden."

I shouldn't have told him, Stone thought. *I put a burden on his shoulders he isn't ready to carry, and he feels its weight pressing down.*

How was he to restore the forests, if he couldn't leave the cavern? All too often had Stone heard the complaint. The boy acted as though he was being punished, when all Stone wanted was to keep him safe.

"You've only just learned to heal," Stone pointed out. "There is time enough to learn more before we hazard the outside world."

Crier groaned, got up and began to pace.

"I am ready," he said. "I know you disagree, but I am. What difference will a few years make? Humans don't live all that long, you know. Glim said so."

"Could you kill me?" Stone asked. He opened an eye

and leveled it at the young Warden. "Friendship aside, if I went absolutely mad and you had no other choice, could you kill me?" Before Crier could stammer an answer, Stone went on, "Because there are creatures out there far worse than I, much larger and fiercer than you can imagine. They may not frighten you, but they terrify me."

"I'm not saying we should go explore," he said in a pleading tone. "I just want to talk to the great tree, talk to that forest, retrieve the egg and come home. It won't take more than a day."

"It's too dangerous," Glim said from the branches above and stepped out from shadow. "You don't know what you're asking. The conclave hasn't forgotten, and they certainly haven't abandoned that tree." She caught and held Crier's attention with a firm look. "It's not worth the risk."

Stone shifted his bulk. "The egg may no longer be there. If conclave agents found the great tree, they may have seen past the illusion and gone down to the hidden chamber."

"They could have taken it," Glim conjectured, "to lure you to them at some point. Or they could have left it and set a trap."

"So we'll be careful!" Crier threw up his arms, as if their worries were unwarranted.

Glim vanished and reappeared below in an instant, her shadow blade in hand and forced Crier back against a tree. The inky weapon pressed to his neck, its tendrils and wisps licked along his flesh like nighttime fire.

"These are dangerous people!" Glim said firmly, not trying to scare him but to prove a point. She let fall the blade into nothing, eased off and set him free. When she spoke next, her voice was soft, a pleading of her own. "They want you, Crier, even more than they want me. And that's saying a lot." He stood taller but still seemed a child before her. "We're here, in this cavern, because we can't protect you. Not from the conclave. We need you to grow stronger, so you can protect yourself."

"How am I supposed to do that here?" Crier asked. "I need more than...this," he said and indicated the trees. "Without a Warden to teach me, I need something that belonged to them. A tree, the egg, a book. Anything."

"You need to give yourself time," Stone said. "Eralle has been in ruin since before you were hatched. It can wait a little longer."

"Fine," Crier said. He was angry, shook off Glim's attempt to comfort him and headed back for his tree. "I'll wait a little longer," he called back over a shoulder, "but I won't wait forever."

* * *

Stone slept on a wide circle of rock before the tunnel, one smoothed over time by breath and scale. The close proximity allowed him to both protect the cavern and sense the lilting blues of winter wind pass between the mountains. The nearby shallow pool and its stream sent out their trickling, a dulcet intermixture of icy song. The first snow had begun to fall, and its crisp touch had left a layer of brittle frost within the passage.

Glim was too tricky to leave a trail, though. Her travel through shadow had left no trace but faint calls, the resounding murmurs of her magic as she went. Hers was different from Crier's, as his was from the conclave agents and theirs from the illusions in the great tree. It was as if every magic had a distinct voice, despite the hushed whispers. They were impossible to understand but not as difficult to tell apart.

Stone had expected her to return with the egg, but when she surfaced from shadow on the other end of the pond, she stood quiet but emptyhanded.

"Have they moved it?" Stone asked.

It wouldn't have surprised him if they had. With all the magic at their disposal, the conclave would have had no trouble seeing past both illusions in the great tree. The egg no longer held magic, but they must have known the Warden it had hatched might one day return for it.

Glim was a bit startled by his voice but walked over to keep from waking Crier.

"No," she replied, "it's still there. I'm just not able to move it through shadow. I've been practicing," she said and shook her head. Golden curls spilled out from her braids and across her shoulders like a sunfall. "It's just too big."

"You didn't see anyone? No traps?"

"Not as far as I could tell," she said. "The forest was empty. The tree was drained to stone, and everything in the chamber had blackened."

Did feys feed on plants as well? He'd seen Glim eat fruits and nuts, but she'd never drained a plant or vine of life the way she had a tree.

Stone considered her words.

"Did you enter the chamber through shadow," he asked, "or did you walk down the passage?"

"Shadow." Her eyes narrowed. "You think they laid traps, and I somehow bypassed them?"

"Anything is possible." Stone shifted his bulk. "I'll just have to go see."

"You're going?" Glim asked in surprise. "What about all your talk of it being too dangerous?"

Stone gave her a pointed look. "You seemed to share the sentiment, but that didn't stop you. Besides," he said and stretched open his wings, "I worry he'll do something rash, like sneak off during the night." Stone had already sensed Crier hiding in the bushes far behind to the right.

He had a satchel with food, a skin filled with water and a staff harnessed across his back. Stone glanced in his direction. "Isn't that right?"

Crier stepped from the bushes and approached with a sullen face. Notch shambled alongside him.

"You'd risk your own life," the boy accused, "but not mine?"

"Crier," Glim said in disappointment, "what were you thinking?"

Stone said to him, "Mine is less a risk. If I fall, you'll still have Glim. You were right," he added, before the boy could voice complaint. "You need more than we can offer. If you think the egg can help you learn anything about the Wardens, then I'll go fetch it for you. But make no mistake. I will never risk your life or allow you to either."

Notch crackled and creaked in his odd manner of speech, ruffled his leaves for good measure.

"I know," Crier said to the treeling. To Stone, he said, "I can learn more from the great tree. The Wardens hid me there for a reason. I understand and appreciate all you two have done and still do for me. But I am not that helpless child anymore. You say you won't let me risk my life. Life *is* risk. I could just as easily die climbing a tree for a piece of fruit than I can against a dragon outside the cavern. You have these expectations, saved me because of them. None of what you hope I can do will come easy. I only know I can't do it alone," he said and looked to them both with affection, "and we have to start somewhere."

"What if we all—" Glim began.

"I'll take you," Stone said to Crier, "but at the first sign of danger, we turn back. No arguments."

"Alright," Crier said slowly, more from surprise than hesitation.

"You'll do as I say," Stone added, "without pause or objection." Crier nodded, still shocked but smiling wider.

"The treeling stays."

Notch ruffled in protest.

"Yes," Crier agreed and gave his companion a pat in apology, "of course. Whatever you say."

Stone lowered his neck for them to climb on.

– 8 –

Morning was still a few hours off. The mountaintops and craggy edges were highlighted in piercing violet, a series of chill lines that softened into shadow. Wind blew from behind, swept up into his wings and carried them when he allowed. It sent flecks of whistling cold out into a swirling panorama and down to a growing layer of pale silence. It was as if the cover of snow was just as hungry as he and sought to feed off every sound.

Stone flew low to the ground, glided by rocks without sounding or thumping a tail. This wasn't a hunt, and he could already sense the empty warrens and abandoned tunnels close to the surface. With the coming of winter's touch, prey had burrowed further down to escape the cold.

The closest lair to the south was two hours out and another over. Stone recalled the claimed areas from last he scouted the range and purposely skirted that one's edge. He was surprised to find faded sense of the larger dragon and flew in for a closer look. The further he went, the more confused he became.

Either he's found a better lair or was slain while out

hunting. Stone paused and turned back before reaching the lair, a wide cave with two entrances, access to water beneath the rocks and the warmth of a lava vent. *Why hasn't another claimed it?*

Something gnawed at his middle, apprehension like an extra sense. It took time to check other lairs along the way, but Stone knew something was wrong from the very first. The closer he drew toward the forest, the more faded was each of their sense and sign. It had to be a single predator. There were too many gone from their lairs, killed or driven out, and those far more deadly than he. What else but another dragon could do such a thing? Stone began to fear they were headed into danger.

"What's wrong?" Crier asked. He sat on a ridge just behind Stone's right ear. "I can always tell when you're bothered. Does it have anything to do with those empty caves we flew past?"

"Maybe," Stone said, deep in thought. Could there be a creature more deadly than a dragon? "Have you heard the whispers of Warden magic or caught the sense of a forest?"

Glim had tied herself in place and was resting with a cheek against his scales. Crier was held fast by lengths of twined spider silk wrapped all the way around. Reins, Glim had called them.

"Magic is more like a feeling," Crier said, "like when light from the sun touches my face, except it's inside, around my heart. I haven't felt anything but sadness since we left. There's no life out here. No trees, no plants, no flowers. How long has it been like this?"

Stone snorted. "For as long as I can remember."

"What's that?" Crier asked and pulled on the corded silk, nudging Stone west. "From that direction. Can you feel it?"

"I don't like when you do that," Stone said and swept

sideways between two outcroppings, "and all I sense is my own irritation."

"It's not magic," Crier said. "It's more like...suffering, a cry for help. It feels awful. You can't sense anything?"

"No," Stone replied, and the unease in his middle grew. "If you're certain, we should fly around it."

The boy leaned forward and shivered.

"They need help," he said. "Can we take a look, just to see what's happening?"

"Remember our agreement."

Stone pulled up short and kept his place in air. He didn't need to turn west, had caught sense of them in a rush of strained emotion and rancid color. He gritted his teeth against it and fought down the knot in his chest. It was the missing dragons, all of them in one place. The sense of death and dying rode the earth with a cloying grasp, even fought against the wind and held strong.

Glim woke as Stone eased them closer to the vale. He had to know what sort of dragon could fell so many in so short a time. Was it his mother? Had she become bored of his hiding and took out her frustration on every other in her path? What would she say when she saw him fully grown and still alive despite her efforts?

"Is something wrong?" Glim asked.

"Yes," Crier said and shifted for a better view, "but we don't know what just yet."

Stone knew before the vale came into sight, flew in to its outer edge and landed on a granite shelf. Between two rocky hills, within its barren recess, were dragons of all manner of shape and size. Wings shattered and torn, bodies bloody and crippled, each had been left to starve and draw in new prey. In a winding circle about the fetid pond at the valley center, tens upon tens lay broken across the rocks. Only a handful had been slain, stripped bare to the bone. All the way on the other side, a few hundred wingspans away, a small fire blazed with spitted dragon meat upon it.

A humanoid stepped out from a covering of scales, as if he had used dragon flesh to forge a home. He stood twice Crier's height, with a chest three times as wide. He had no hair or ears to speak of, and his head flared out and back into three segments of dark bone. With a prominent brow, a flatted nose like two slits and horns jutting out from his chin, the creature looked nothing like a human but for his two arms and legs. His body was adorned with scarce garments of scale, had colored markings and scars from head to foot.

The hunter walked past his cooking fire and pulled a length of dragon bone from the ground. Carved from a talon, with one end in jagged barbs, it looked to be the sort of weapon to tear and rend.

It's not water, Stone realized, sickened to his core. He looked down at the rotten pool, its stench an acrid cry. *It's blood.*

The hunter threw his spear.

Though he knew the distance was too great, that the spear could never hit, Stone turned and moved to flee. He spread his wings and pushed off as jarring whispers carried the weapon. It tore clean through. The membrane of his right wing parted at the center in a surge of pain and blood.

How? was all Stone could think, as he stumbled on all fours and tried to right his gait. The length of shaped bone had struck and pierced halfway through a rock. It fell apart into smoky vapors. Stone sensed it reappear in the hunter's hand. *Magic!*

Stone regained his balance and continued at a run. He pushed off but had trouble staying aloft. He'd flown with an injured wing before, but this wound felt different, as if the spear had struck something vital. It was already beginning to heal, tingling at the shredded edges, but the hunter was chasing after as well. If he cleared the valley ridge, and Stone was still in sight—

"Turn!" Crier shouted and pulled hard to the left on the silken cord.

Stone tucked his wing out of reflex and shifted to the left. The spear still grazed his closed wing, whistled past to a grizzled chorus of hushed and echoed chanting. It split the ground where it stuck, a dozen wingspans ahead, and again broke apart into ashen wisps.

Warden magic sang out in a burst of soothing fire. It reached across and touched his wing, spread up along each vein, pulled taut the severed ligaments and mended the tattered breach. A pair of airlings stepped out from two swirls of swollen wind. They caught Stone beneath the wings and helped him push off. Within a few beats, they were far above the ground.

The dragon hunter fell away and out of sense.

* * *

Stone had been frantic but grew calmer as they flew. He'd never seen or heard tale of anything like the hunter, nor the magic that imbued that grisly weapon. Stone had been in hiding for years to avoid his mother but still went out to scout the range from time to time. Could so much have changed in so short a span? And what of his cruel mother? Was she among the broken bodies waiting to bleed out or be slaughtered? Had the hunter already feasted upon her flesh or even fashioned his spear from her bones? Or was she behind it all? Had she somehow brought the hunter near to where Stone was last seen? Was it all just an attempt to find him, to lure him out of hiding?

Not likely, Stone thought. *He was too formidable, even*

for mother. He couldn't imagine her sitting idly by with so much meat for the taking. *Unless they served a purpose, drawing in more and more prey with the sense of blood and carrion.* That many living dragons in one place, wounded or not, would have sent lesser creatures fleeing or into hiding. *It was only reckless curiosity that drew me in.*

"We have to go back," Crier said and looked behind toward the vale. "We can't just leave them to suffer."

Stone pressed on toward the forest. He didn't want to risk turning back home so soon, for fear of leading the hunter to them. He had no way of knowing what other sort of magic the hunter possessed. Could he track them in air? That bone spear had tasted Stone's blood. Could the magic that imbued it lead the hunter to him? Nothing was impossible where magic was concerned. He needed to fly further off, far away from the cavern, before turning back. The forest was close enough that the trip wouldn't have been wasted. Stone planned to grab the egg, shake the hunter from his sense and return home without delay.

"We almost died," Glim said sharply. Her body flush against his, Stone could feel her heart still beating a pale rhythm. "And you want to risk our lives going back? How many times can we discuss this? There are no other dragons like Stone. Even near death, they're lethal. And the one with the spear? He was a krag *and* a mage. We'd fare better against the conclave."

"All life is worth saving," Crier said, more to Stone. "What if it'd been you lying there, in terrible pain, waiting to die?"

"It nearly was," Stone replied.

He refused to hear any more of it, kept on without word or acknowledgment of complaint. Two more hours through falling snow, they passed beyond another valley and the infertile remnants of a lake. A bed of cracked earth and salted rock, all life had been stripped away.

He was unsure what could've caused it. The stories he'd been told were proven false time and again. Whether it was dragon fire, wild magic gone awry or a combination of both, the water and its unlucky inhabitants had long ago been boiled to a lifeless mud. What remained was a scorched echo of a time when life thrived.

It was typical of the world his kind had wrought, the parched land scarred by fire, the desolation of warring magic. He'd inherited their destruction, a forlorn legacy of dragons.

What will I leave behind? he wondered, as they swept wide to the east and circled low into the forest.

Stone purposely entered where the grandwoods were sparse, between rugged slips of oak and ironhorn, the knotted faces of heartwood and split crowns of blood ash. He slowed to a safe beat, let the lower currents carry him through. If the hunter could track them, he certainly hadn't kept pace. Only memory of his attack seemed to follow. Stone's main concern now was of the conclave.

He chose to approach the great tree from an area he'd rarely traveled, uncertain of what he'd find. Glim had been away from the Hollow for too long, had no way of knowing if the conclave still searched for the Warden who had brought life to their forest.

Even if they wasted little time in extinguishing it. He landed a good distance off from their old home, within sense but out of sight. The whispers had already started, the open calling of Warden magic, the embrace beneath its hush. Unfortunately, they were not alone. Another set of voices joined the tumult in his mind, secretive and dark, subtle and accusing. *Fey magic?*

It was different from what he remembered of their weapons, the harsh tones with purpose. These few tried to remain hidden. They burrowed in the earth, clung to frozen roots and laid in wait like a predator.

"There are traps ahead," Crier said, his hand against a tree. A flicker of life and renewed wood had sprung up beneath his touch. "I don't know exactly where."

"I do."

Stone followed each whisper in his mind, saw them in cloying mist, murky vapors that pooled and swirled in blacks and grays. He moved closer between trees and clawed up a handful of snowy earth. Perhaps he could set them off from a safe distance.

"Be careful," Glim warned.

She loosened the cords holding her fast, held on with one hand and drew a shadow blade to the other.

"We are the only ones here," Stone said.

"How do you know there are traps?" she asked Crier. "Can you speak with the trees?"

"Only when I touch them," he replied. "They're not dead, just severely weakened."

The great tree came into sight, much the same as they had left it but for the shattered branches in a jagged pile and blackened debris strewn within. Every vine he had placed far above had been fed upon and snapped. It made him wonder how the feys could have reached so high and across so many trees. He'd never seen Glim use her wings for more than carrying her across the ground. She could reach the lower branches but never went all that much higher. Perhaps her translucent wings were not strong enough to bear her weight at such heights.

Or she's never felt the need to ride the winds as I do. Stone avoided the magic left further out from the great tree and eyed those placed beyond the illusory opening. *What if they're not traps meant to harm,* he considered, *but an alarm of sorts, like how Glim had set little silver bells on a silken string upon her snares? Setting off a trap could alert the conclave to our presence.*

Instead, he tossed a trail of earth between the swirls of

magic, marking a path toward the entrance.

"Don't stray from it," he told them as Glim and Crier climbed down. "Get the egg and come straight back. It's not safe to stay."

"If I could just talk to it," Crier said in awe of the great tree.

Glim pulled him gently along. "There's no time for that right now. Let's just get what we came for."

Stone waited as the two passed through illusion and went inside. He may have been able to force himself down the tunnel but saw no reason to risk it. The last thing they needed was for him to get stuck and have to claw his way back out, possibly losing or destroying the egg in the process. No, it was better if they dragged—

A burst of yellow shook his ears, as Glim cried out and was muffled. Stone sensed them all appear before he could move toward the entrance. They were fey, twenty-three males and seven females. It was like they had been masked within the magic, the way Glim hid in shadow. He hadn't sensed them before, though. It was as if they weren't actually there until the instant that they were.

Nets had gone up the moment feys appeared. Stone wasted no time in thought but pushed off and twisted. He grabbed one of the silken meshes with his mouth and tossed it, swatted another aside and was already in air as angry curses followed after. Enchanted arrows and magic fire shrieked past, lit the forest around him in crackling silver and streaming flares of golden purple. Branches gave way to heated shards, rained down in his wake and elicited another round of irate curses.

There were four more feys in the chamber far below, but he couldn't get a full sense of their struggle before he rose. He had no choice but to trust in the two to take care of themselves for the time being. Glim had both the shadow and her swords, had trained Crier with a staff.

They just needed to hold off being captured until he could get to them.

"The dragon's fled," he heard a male say into an orb of crystal. It was the one with the icy sword, who had led the first attack all those years ago.

I should have killed him, Stone thought as he reached the forest top and turned about.

"He has not," a female warned through the orb.

Stone sounded the treetops with a beat, chose the weakest and sped toward it. Wings pulled in tight, he shouldered through and took aim on another. It joined the cacophony of rolling gray and pointed black wailing toward the ground. It tore at branches and stripped them free, further shattered forest bones into a storm of dust and death. Magic shields went up in flashes of hurried shock and harsh whispers. Not all were in time but were snuffed beneath the gale, their violet flares extinguished to bloody ruin.

Feys shouted their grief and outrage, scattered upon wings or crawled free of the rubble. Stone had followed the debris down and let loose fire as he passed. Bile clung to rock and flesh, sticky flames that would not abate. More screams rang out, the pulsing reds of pain and torment. He felt the magic of enchanted arrows cut through the air behind. Using grandwoods for cover, he turned sharply to the left, sped upward and spiraled back.

"Get the boy up here!" the lead fey ordered. Two with swords headed inside the great tree, while the remaining archers and mages tried to strike Stone from the sky. "I know you can hear me, dragon! Surrender yourself now, or your master dies!"

Stone knew it for a trick. They wouldn't kill the only Warden, but neither could he allow them to know that he cared.

They might not kill him, Stone thought, *but they'd*

certainly hurt or even maim him. I don't think I could bear that.

Glim slipped from shadow behind an archer on the outskirts of their ranks. She kicked out one of his legs and caused him to loose his arrow. It shot like a bolt of lightning into the shoulder of a female mage across the way. Glim then struck him across the back of his head with the pommel of a shadow blade. He collapsed into a heap, and she disappeared back into shadow. Stone feared her unwillingness to kill would be her undoing.

Feys still struggled to douse the flames, tore clothes off before it spread, splashed water from skins, rolled franticly in the snow or swatted at it with gloved hands. Some even used magic, called frost up to freeze the fire in place.

Stone ignored them and headed straight for the lead fey. He landed before the agent and shook the ground with his bulk. The fey didn't flinch, held tight his icy sword and stared back with disdain. Six others carried Crier out from the illusory opening, the boy kicking and fighting the entire way.

There was no holding back for Stone's ruse to work. He clicked his back teeth and unleashed the full extent of his breath. He let loose a few scale lengths to Crier's right, so the flame wouldn't strike him. He might suffer damage from the heat, but the boy would survive long enough to heal himself later. Stone was relying on the hope the feys wanted Crier alive at all cost.

Contempt turned to shocked confusion, as the lead fey leapt aside. A hasty magic shield went up in a violet half-shell of shimmer. One fey twisted to cover Crier with his body. A continuous stream of deadly fire, its torrent splashed over the shield and wavered the air between them, melted snow and ice, blistered flesh and ignited clothing of the two caught outside the protective magic.

Once Stone heard the whispers begin to fail, he relented and took wing.

The lead fey was burned over half his body but still alive, crawling weakly toward the snow. Two agents were fallen over, cracked open and bloodied, smoking like cooked meat. The remaining four grabbed hold of Crier and carried him away.

The boy was unharmed.

Stone's gamble had paid off. He could attack now without worrying they'd threaten Crier to stop him. He circled a grandwood and landed among the few feys still strong enough to fight back. Only nine remained, their fellows dead, unconscious or severely wounded. Glim had continued to harass them from the shadows and knew to stay out of Stone's way.

Arrows and magic bolts sped toward him. Secure in the knowledge his wounds would heal, Stone was less afraid than caution warranted. He could focus his senses on the magic sent his way, dodge aside or tuck a wing as he moved closer. The few hits that scorched along a ridge or the outer bone of a wing had caused pain but were not enough to deter his course.

He roared when a sliver of magic slammed into his chest, a slip of purple light that blossomed between two scales. Stone swung his tail in a rage, tore through half a heartwood and sent petrified shards cascading out. With a narrowed gaze toward the female mage, he stormed toward her without care for the frenzied barrage that tried to halt him.

"Rory!" she screamed to the male archer backing away beside her, his wings fluttering in fear. "Help me!"

Stone was agile for his size and had the benefit of perfect sense. He knew exactly where each attack came from, which ones he could avoid or turn aside and the ones he could only mitigate. Those he let hit were minor strikes, caused little to no damage or as little as he could manage. Still, each one hurt and only angered him further.

The mage turned and tried to fly off, but Stone was quicker. He lunged, caught her upper body in his maw and killed her with a single shake. Despite the rumbling in his stomach, he let her body fall and leapt after the nearby archer. An arrow grazed his neck at the same time one struck a shoulder. He had no choice but to let one of the magic missiles pierce his side. Any other twist of his body would have caused the arrow at his neck to strike deeper in.

Glim took down another mage as Stone leapt. The fey archer had abandoned his bow and taken wing. Stone caught him by the feet. While he was careful not to bite all the way through, the fey's bones were too fragile not to break. He screamed an anguished pale, his hopeless fear given voice. Stone thrashed him against a tree, bent and broke him to pieces contained within flesh. A second thrash for good measure, and he tossed the fey aside.

The others had fled, cost him minutes to track and kill. When he returned to the great tree, he found Glim all alone.

"Where's Crier?" she asked in a fearful tone that said she had expected them to return together.

How did I lose track of him? Stone cursed himself for giving in to the bloodlust of battle. *The one with the icy sword must have him.*

"I don't sense anyone else," he said, "nor any magic but the tree. Where would they have taken him?"

Glim didn't reply right away. She seemed to struggle with her emotions and blinked away tears before she spoke.

"I'm sorry," she said. "I should've been watching—"

"We're both sorry, but we need to move if we're going to catch them. They would've taken him to the Hollow, yes? Which way is it?"

She nodded and climbed his neck. "Northwest, past the grove of ironhorn. There's a crevice—"

Stone was off with such speed she was forced to hug a ridge to keep from falling and hooked both her feet behind the next. Trees went by in a blur of sense, in the dark of fading day. Shadows at the forest floor had grown long across the boles and stretched off like a starless night. He caught sense of the four as a large opening ahead dipped down beyond his reach. It was as if the ground had been cracked open, like a split in the earth no bigger than a dozen wingspans but of a depth so far down it seemed to grow deeper the closer they drew toward it. Two feys flew side by side, carried Crier between them, while a third rushed ahead.

"I have them," Stone said and pushed even harder.

He slipped down through the crevice, into the dark of earth. They were just a few beats away when the harsh clarion call of magic rang out at both sides. They were moving too fast when he first heard the whispers. There was no time to react, and the spell had been sprung. A forked spark of silver branched out from both sides of earth and rock, met in the tunnel's middle and struck them full force. Stone felt his heart cease beating in the same moment every muscle tensed. He felt frozen in air, petrified like the trees. They struck the ground and slid, slipping further into darkness.

– 9 –

Stone woke to gnawing pain and the clamor of fey magic. Its insidious whispers were like claws in his ears, scraping away at his mind and clouding his perfect sense. Everything was forced apart, the colored smells from his vision, the vibrant sounds from his touch, and all he could taste was the defeat of his own blood. No longer could he experience the world around him as a single image. His flawless perception had been fractured and with it his sense of self.

Negative emotion began to overwhelm him, driven by cloying murmurs. He was slowly drowning in the dark of loneliness and despair, the loss and lies throughout his life, the death and disappointment. The hushed voices were relentless. They tore away at his will, his worth, and left shreds in their wake.

It was only pain that pulled him from the dread long enough to remember others needed him. He didn't have time for despair. He tried to move and nearly roared from the agony.

His wings had been maimed, their membranes cut away. All that remained of them were bloodied bones and shorn scales along the ridges. The tendons in all four limbs had been severed and could no longer bear his weight. He tried to sound with his tail, but heavy metal chains made it impossible to move. They encased and imprisoned him, crushing downward with their bulk. Even his jaw had been shackled closed, limiting his view to a single direction.

Beneath him seemed a circle of carved rock. Magic thrummed upward from its markings along with winter chill. His chains were moored there and carried through to large pillars. Those were shaped as well, adorned with enchanted patterns. They reached beyond his view up into darkness. Past those was a stone table, dimly lit by candles, and upon its surface were a multitude of metal tools and bloodied instruments.

My blood, he realized.

He could see a wall in the distance and understood why the fey voices nearby were all muffled. Buildings, they were called, lairs constructed by hand rather than nature. Humans had raised thousands of them, stacking den upon den until the giant structures reached as tall as trees. Not one had withstood the might of dragonfire. This one would be no different...if he could pry open his maw.

I have to find Glim, he thought and struggled to break free. The pain kept him focused, kept his mind from darker thoughts. Whatever magic was at play, it was wreaking havoc on his mind. *There's no telling how much time has passed*, he reasoned, *but she can't be far. It's also unlikely they've imprisoned her in the same place as Crier. They want him alive.* A very dark thought crossed his mind. *Would they have killed her? They've been trying to kill her for years. Why stay their hand now?* He tried to shake his head and growled in frustration when it wouldn't move. *No, they'll use her to control him, to force Crier to do their bidding.*

Just like they'll use me.

Two male feys went flying past, just outside the candlelight. They carried between them a third, one slumped and without a heartbeat. Stone could smell his breath upon the corpse. There was no joy in that one's death, but he would burn them all to save Crier.

A female entered shortly after and approached from behind the table. She seemed older than Glim, with a touch of silver to her braids and timeworn etchings near her eyes. She wore a silk robe, purple at the shoulders and black down to her sandals. It was tied about the waist with a delicate length of golden chain. There was magic about her, in her movements, in her clothing, in the crystals hanging from her belt.

"Comfortable, I trust?" It was the female voice from battle, the one on the other end of the crystal orb. She'd spoken to the lead fey with authority at the time. Was she in charge of the conclave? Or even all of the fey? "We've gone to a great deal to secure your presence. I hope there are no hard feelings."

Whispers clung to every word, rode them through his ears like invaders laying siege. There was promise within them, images of freedom and open skies if he just obeyed. He could have everything he'd ever wanted, anything he could imagine, if only he'd submit.

"Where's the boy?" Stone demanded.

She narrowed her eyes, as if she were both surprised and perturbed. Her hand was clasped about a crystal from her belt. She seemed to consider Stone anew while thumbing its smooth surface.

"And Glim?" he went on. It was difficult to speak. His throat was hoarse and terribly dry. It felt like it'd been days since last he drank. "What have you done with them?"

The fey ignored his questions. She began to study

him instead with an appraising touch, making note of his unusual markings.

"Black ridge with gray heart," she said in admiration, fingers trailing his neck, "and minimal spacing. Very few lines share that coloring." Stone tried in vain to kill her, to silence the pervasive whispers. The chains held him fast. "Such a prominent foretalon. I wonder," she said, lips close enough to feel her breath, "what magnificent specimen sired you. I have my suspicions. Perhaps you could tell me. Do you know his name?"

Despite the magic assaulting his mind and senses, Stone could feel each wound slowly healing. He would need to act before the fey noticed. It would take far too long for his wings to fully mend but not so much for his limbs. If he was willing to push his body to the extreme, to endure the pain and inevitable damage, he might be able to break free of the chains and strike. The new wounds would eventually heal. More importantly, he'd be free.

He just needed to distract her, to keep her thoughts occupied and eyes focused anywhere but on his injuries.

"Come face me," he said, mentally struggling to fend off her magic, "if you wish to talk." Seemingly amused, she moved to stand before him, ice-blue eyes upon his. "What have you done with the others?"

"You mean the Warden," she said, as if to emphasize she knew exactly what Crier was. Her mouth curled into a grin. "And the Shadow Walker."

Stone heard another fey approach before he saw the male step out from darkness. He carried with him a dark box, fashioned of hardened clay.

"Magister Sorrel," he said to her quietly, with respect, with fear, "the item you requested."

She accepted it and dismissed him with barely a nod. He bowed and took wing back outside, relieved to be away, though from which of the two was unclear. She could barely contain her elation, as she opened the box. A new chorus of whispers flooded out, filling the room with the gentle coaxing of Warden magic.

By the sounds echoed back, Stone gauged the walls around him. Whatever building they were in, it was both wider and taller than himself at full height by three times. Did that mean they were in one of the fey cities? If so, how had they brought him here? He had no idea how large a city was or how he might search its buildings for Glim and Crier.

Focus! None of that mattered if he couldn't break free, couldn't rid himself of the whispers inhibiting his sense. What if I try something different?

"If you agree to let us go," Stone offered, "I'll tell you the location of a thriving forest. You and your people could feed upon trees once again."

Sorrel pulled a polished wooden circlet from the chest, its redwood gleaming in the light. She placed it upon her head, so that its single green gem rested above her brow.

"You will tell me everything," she promised, "whether you want to or not. You can rest assured of that." She closed the box and placed it upon the table. When her eyes met his again, they were accompanied with a swarm of hushed cries and soft demands. "Now, who is your sire?"

Stone could feel the strength of the circlet's magic wash over his scales, but its prodding was just a tingle at the back of his mind. He considered not answering, just to test its power. He wanted to keep her talking, however, keep her attention on their conversation. He was already able to flex his claws without too much pain. A little longer, and he might be healed enough to bear his own weight.

"I never knew him," he replied at last, "and mother never spoke of him. It's not uncommon for dragons to mate and never see each other again."

The Magister nearly laughed. "Is that so?" Her look of mirth at his expense was infuriating. "Who told you this?"

His growl shook the chains across his maw. *More lies! Why? What was the point of it all?*

"I see," she said, surmising her own answer. "What other tales has your mother told you, I wonder. And who was she, this paragon of truth?" Her voice hardened with the touch of whispers. "What was she called?"

Though she had never told them directly, he and his sister had overheard their mother speak her name only once. It was right before she took the life of a female who had flown too close to their lair. Mother had claimed she could sense the newly hatched eggs upon the other. By her given name, she had vowed to track the nest and destroy all the offspring for the slight.

"Stormcry," Stone answered with shame, though he wasn't sure why. His mother had been cruel, a savage killer of all who crossed her path, but so was every other dragon or creature he'd encountered in his life. Surviving was hard. It made killers of them all.

Sorrel's wings fluttered.

"I *knew* you were special." There was triumph in her words. "You have no idea who he is," she went on, "who he was, your father. He started it all, struck a bargain to kill the Wardens and set dragons free." She clucked her tongue with recrimination. "Well, free to burn the world and doom us all."

"No." Stone tried to shake his head in disbelief. This was some ploy. She wanted something from him, though he couldn't discern what.

"Ebonclaw," the Magister said and stepped forward, her touch once again upon his maw. If only he could open—"He was one of the first, an ancient, born of Warden magic. I imagine they never suspected their creation would find a way to undo them all. Where is he now?"

"I don't know," Stone forced a reply out through his teeth, straining against the chains for a gap large enough to loose his breath. "I never met him."

"Where is Stormcry?"

He closed tight his eyes against the whispers. Their assault was unending, a whirlwind in his mind that refused to abate.

"She cast me out when I was five." He could barely hear the words, was still dazed by the revelation. His father had ruined the world. Something in him knew it to be the truth. "I haven't seen her since."

"Five," Sorrel repeated. She was either surprised or disbelieving. "What did you do? Why would she send you away from her protection at such a young age?"

"I—I didn't do anything." *Did I?* he wondered. *Did she force me to leave because of something I did?*

"You must tell me," the fey insisted, green gem upon her brow flashing. "What did you do?"

Stone growled again with ferocity, pulled against his bonds. Bile slipped between his teeth, dripped over the enchanted rock beneath him. His tendons were nearly healed.

"Tell me!" Sorrel's growing frustration was turning to anger, reddening her cheeks. "You cannot resist the maker's bond."

Steam rose up from his nostrils. He'd ignited the bile while still in his mouth. He glared at the fey, put the full of his weight upon his claws and labored against the chains. He mouthed a stifled roar and heard it echo back among the cries of distant screams within the city. Metal links began to protest, stretched across his back.

"Impossible," Sorrel said, wide-eyed and in fear. She backed away out of instinct. "What are you?"

Another roar in the distance, and one of the chains

about his neck came apart in a shower of links. Scales across his back shattered beneath the continued force. Hide cracked and split. Muscles parted and tore. Bones creaked and shattered.

A male fey came rushing in.

"Magister Sorrel!" He said and halted abruptly midair at the sight of Stone breaking free. Gripped with fear, he strained to report, "We're under attack. Another dragon. The city—" he pulled his eyes from Stone and focused them on Sorrel—"it's on fire.

With a final effort, Stone roared the chains around his maw apart. Breath fountained from his mouth and splattered sticky flames across the ground. Some struck the enchanted circle beneath him and hissed, while other droplets struck both fey and elicited screams. He stood amidst the din of metal links and broken magic raining down upon them.

Sorrel frantically grasped for a blue gem hanging about her waist, while the other dropped to the ground in vocal agony. Terrified, kept upright by wing alone, the Magister conjured ice to douse her flesh. It crackled and blackened her cheek and a shoulder, left holes in her silk robes and quieted some of the whispers.

Free but near collapse, broken and bloodied, Stone knew his only chance was to strike fast. Debris fell from above in streams that blinded and choked. The entire structure seemed to shake with the throbbing of his vision. Pushed beyond endurance, he dropped to all fours. He planned to end them in fire but could barely remain conscious.

The Magister turned to flee, unconcerned with her subordinate. Rocks began to fall in a deadly torrent across the floor. Stone drew back to loose his breath, when a roar not his own tore through the surrounding structure. The wall in front tumbled down, a cascade of boulders and debris. A stream of fire struck the feys from the opening. It left nothing in its wake but their ashes and the Warden crown.

A massive dragon stepped through the dying flames. She stared down upon Stone, her piercing gaze filled with madness. Stone's heart skipped a beat. Frozen in shock, his mind and body nearly spent, he'd expected to see his mother. What stood before him, however, was...

"Willow?"

– 10 –

"Admit it!" Willow shouted down at her brother. Fire dripped from her maw in gobs, wild spittle as she spoke. "You left me to die, *over* and *over* again. Why?" Her voice was strained, tormented. "I loved you. I thought you loved me!"

Stone was stricken into silence, so dumbfounded he could scarcely believe his sister stood before him. She'd died in his arms! How could she be here? Had he already lost consciousness? Was this a fevered dream?

Distant cries of the dying and the echoed crackle of flames were fading, but voices could be heard drawing closer. Commands were given in harsh tones. Soled feet wrapped against the stones.

"I knew mother would eventually turn you against me," she went on, shaking her head at painful memories, unmindful of the scene around her. "But torture? I was never sure how you knew." She looked down upon his stupor, tears turning into steam across her snout. "But you did. I see it now. You somehow *knew* I would heal." Her gaze narrowed to his mending wings. "Just as you do."

Arrows struck her side. More voices rang out as feys took to the air. Willow hadn't flinched as the barbs pierced her hide. She swiped an arm across them, severing the embedded shafts. With a roar that shook the ground, she turned her head and filled the air with a storm of whirling fire. Feys screamed and fell, their whispers of magic forever silenced. A swipe of her tail ended more, smashed through rocks and bones alike. The few that remained were impaled by a wing tip and tossed aside. She loomed over the building, a vision of death become flesh.

How had she grown so large? Stone's eyelids began to waver, as welcomed slumber took firmer hold.

"No you don't," Willow said and angrily grabbed him by the throat. He was fractured, broken open, but still an adult. She held him up for inspection as if he were but a hatchling. "You've spent a lifetime avoiding me. No more. Do you hear me?" She gave a rough shake to wake him further. "No more!"

I don't understand. Stone tried to speak, but all that came out were incoherent gurgles.

Willow tossed him across the floor, sent him skidding over broken links and fallen rock. She brought a foot crashing down upon the enchanted circle of stonework he'd been chained to. It cratered beneath the blow like a weaving of cracks and ruptures. Its whispers quieted into a growing, unsettled silence.

"You held me," she said with soft accusation, "while my life drained away. You looked afraid. You were sorry." She smashed her fist through a remaining wall. "You grinned. You laughed. I've remembered it so often, I can't tell which really happened. I only know that you left me, left me to heal, alone in the dark, with their blood and scent all around me, all over me. I was alone still when the hydra's mate returned. He was outraged by what he saw and took that rage out on me."

She can heal? The thought went through his mind repeatedly, like a buried set of whispers. He refused to believe it true, couldn't fathom how it was even possible.

She swallowed hard, fell back on her hind legs. Eyes closed tight against the memory, she sat amidst the ruin and dying fire, body trembling as she spoke.

"I was helpless against him. There was nothing I could do but scream as he fed," she said and laughed, unexpectedly, a terrible sobbing laugh, "as he tore me to pieces. I thought I would die at any moment. I should have. I *wanted* to. But I didn't." She opened her eyes, stared off into nothing. "And he fed. And fed. I healed, and he fed. I was a perpetual feast, maimed and crippled time again."

"He tried to kill me," Willow said with a manic wistfulness, "but it just wouldn't take. He tore my wings off. I watched them rot beside me. I couldn't move, couldn't crawl. He tore those away too. I was meat and nothing more, just like mother always told me." She looked his way and snorted. "I guess, in the end, you believed her too."

"No," Stone managed to croak, blinking furiously to steady his vision. *It's not true.* "That's not—"

"I had no way of knowing how long I was held there," she went on, ignoring her brother's poor attempts at speech, "how many times I was torn apart. I'd cry out for you to save me, to set me free from my nightmare. But you never did." Her short laugh was filled with pain, the sort only a loved one could deliver through betrayal. "I imagined you living your life, without me, having left me to suffer, after I sacrificed myself for you. I played those images in my head, over and over to escape, anything to be away from what was happening. It took a long time for me to realize," she said and nearly choked on the words, "that it's what you wanted all along. I was the weak one and paid the price." Her wing struck the wall nearest Stone, crumbled rocks down upon him. He grunted as they struck and nearly buried him. Her voice filled with spite and anger. "Who's the weak one, now?"

Though his wounds were healing, his wings forming new membranes, the rocks opened new ones. He pushed them aside, struggled for the strength to sit up and explain.

I didn't know. He pleaded in his mind. *How could I?*

"Eventually," Willow said, "a pack of wyverns found the lair. They killed the hydra, tore him apart as he did me." She stood and shook the dust from her wing. "They might not have noticed I was alive if I hadn't laughed. I just couldn't keep it in." She laughed again, a low rumbling that grew and grew until it ended abruptly with a hiss. "They fed upon me without relent, until all I could see each time I woke were bones jutting from my torso. They crushed my heart, over and over, watched it regrow and beat again. Finally, thankfully, one stung me, unloaded all its venom. My organs blackened and withered. My heart stopped and eyes closed."

"I'm so sorry," Stone said. His legs wobbled beneath him, but he managed to stand. "You must believe—"

"I woke later to find them gone. I was alone again," she said and turned his way, "alone in the painful silence of my body slowly mending."

"If I knew—"

"I went back to our lair," she said without listening, "but it was empty."

Empty? He'd never gone back to see her, knew he wasn't welcome. He just assumed their mother would be there.

"Still," Willow said with a cluck of her tongue, "it didn't take long to find you. When I saw you in the distance, my heart soared at the thought of being together again." She suddenly looked crestfallen, as if reliving the moment that followed. "But then it sank at the memory of my torment, what you did to me, what you forced me to endure. I wanted to revisit that torment on you."

No, Stone thought and shook his head in denial. *It was you? This whole time, I thought it was mother...*

"It was no easy task," she said with crazed mirth, "finding just the right predators to send your way. I had to be sure you wouldn't risk the meal. Frightening off potential prey from your path was much simpler. I had to keep you hungry. It became quite the game, staying out of sense, keeping track of yours. I've gotten very good at it."

Stone was trying to understand her reasoning. She'd clearly been devastated, her mind haunted by a past he didn't even know had existed. He simply couldn't grasp why she'd grown to hate him so much. Had her thoughts and memories become so twisted with the imagined? Did she honestly believe in her heart that he'd not only wanted her dead but tortured as well? How could she have come so far from the loving sister he remembered so well?

"But then you up and disappeared," she groused with a huff. "I still don't know where you went off to. If I hadn't lured that hunter north, I don't know if I would have ever found you again!"

"Please listen," he said. "I had no idea you were still alive...or that you could heal. The only reason I can heal is because—"

"Lies!" Willow swept her tail beneath his legs, sent him crashing to one side. She charged forward and was on him in an instant, her claw gripping his throat once again. "You're just like mother. You spew lies as easy as drawing breath. You're as alien to the truth as you are to love. How I ever cared for you, how I was *ever* so weak... Well, I will never be that woeful creature again."

"If you truly believe I could ever hate you," Stone said, emotion catching in his throat, "or if you do indeed hate me, then end my life." He could see her contemplate his death behind the mask of delusion that clouded her eyes. If only he could make her see the truth. "I would rather die than live knowing you don't love me. There is nothing I wouldn't do for you." Her look softened but brow crinkled, as if struggling to align his words with the reality she'd chose to cling to. "I'm so sorry."

Willow roared.

She threw him aside and turned away. She moved to leave but looked back.

"Save your apologies. I'll not hear them from the likes of you."

His sister took wing with such force she caused more rocks to tumble down from the smashed ceiling and what remained of the walls. Stone labored to stand. Most of his wounds had closed, but flight was not an option. He couldn't chase after Willow if he wanted to. Though he did want to, other lives were in danger. If he wanted to find Glim and Crier, he'd have to do it on foot.

* * *

The Hollow was not what Stone expected.

He thought the subterranean world of the feys would have been more akin to a massive cave or series of tunnels. What met him upon exiting the ruined building, however, was a whole other expanse as wide and open as above ground. The entirety of undersky was lit in dulcets of violet twinkle, interspersed with waves of blue and pale echoes of snowy pores. Its call was so high, so far above this second layer of earth, that it may as well have been stars crying out their glowing welcome.

Eroded pillars stretched between, impossibly thin

at the middle. Rotating brightness reinforced them in discernable whispers, sunlight symbols of blazoned power and fey determination. Their haphazard growth all throughout spoke of a time when nature ruled. The distant city of spired buildings declared that time had come and gone.

Like artificial stalags, both -mites and -tites, shaped rock coiled and twisted downward, curved and folded upward, but did not meet between. Their respective tips were adorned in lighted crystal of varied color. Marked banners hung and wavered in the wind. Though there were no clouds to mar the bright of undersky, the tickled ozone of a storm felt ever present.

Shroomdens flowered beyond the city. Stone knew from experience their stalks ranged greatly in width and height, nearly as much as their caps varied in shape. The enormous mushrooms typically dominated any warrens, spreading as far as walls allowed. Here they seemed in check, halted to a forest. A fashioned stream ran through them, cut off from a nearby river. The resonance of its rush revealed a current strangely strong.

Fresh water? Stone surmised by its cerulean aroma and wondered where it came from. There was no river near the great tree. Could there be an entirely separate environment beneath the surface, one that has no ties to the above? Or were they just so very far from the forest they'd left? *Where exactly are we?*

There were creatures penned near a brackish pond, surrounded by pillared walls. Sizeable worms, as lengthy as any fey, clung to leafless plants three times their height. They'd woven ties between the tree-like reeds, akin to the webbing of a spider. Some of the interlaced strands were quite intricate, while others seemed newly formed. The bulbous pulsing at the center of the largest ones must have been cocoons.

The only other life Stone could sense was the feys themselves. They swarmed about the city, fluttering from one spire to the next in a cacophony of chaos. He wasn't sure how those flitting with all speed toward one another didn't collide and crash downward. Those who carried sacks or guided floating platforms might have moved at a slower pace, but they were no more concerned with safety than those dashing through their path. Armed guards were stationed in intervals, watching out from posts upon the towers. A group of them had gathered at the base of one shrouded in whispers. The steady beating of a large drum called even more.

Could he face them if he had to? Did he have any other choice? His wounds were mostly healed but for a few breaks and tears. His wings, though, were not and likely wouldn't be for some time. The membranes were growing back, slowly stretching from ridge to spine. It was alarming how easily he was adapting to the pain. Whether it was a consequence of whatever truly caused him and his sister to heal or from the surety of knowing that he would, it lent a measure of freedom he had never experienced. If he could endure the aches of injury, he would be free from all its harms. As a dragon, he was immortal. Without fear of harm, he was unstoppable.

Is that how Willow had grown so large? he wondered. *By taking on bigger prey or attacking greater numbers, assured she would survive?* He imagined how much larger he'd be had he known the truth sooner. *Assuming I can heal as she does and not just as a result of Crier's magic. She could be playing at another game, hoping to see me become reckless.*

He searched the rubble for the Warden crown, his talons guided by its whisper. When he found the wooden circlet, he slipped it over a wing barb and forced it down to a snug fit. He could live with its low murmurings, found comfort in the Warden magic.

Besides, he thought wryly, *it might come in handy to have a trinket that forces dragons to answer questions. Even if it doesn't work on me.*

He had more questions than time to ask, about his mother, his sister, his ability to heal and why the feys who have experience with dragons were so convinced he was something else. Being a dragon was all he knew. What else would he be?

The armed feys were on the move toward him, led by the one Stone had burned at the great tree. He'd never forget that one's sense. Twelve others took wing with sword and bow, while half as many guided two large weapons upon metal platforms. They looked similar to bows but turned on their side, laid across the floating beds. Buoyed by magic, the heavy weapons moved with ease but at a slower pace than the feys above. No doubt designed to hunt dragons, the great arrows each one loosed would be as spears thrown with deadly strength. Would they be guided by magic as well, as the hunter's bone spear was?

Stone needed a course of action that left none of his enemies alive and gave time enough to heal before more were rallied against him. It wouldn't do to be captured again. There was a chance Willow had stayed behind to watch, but would she rescue him a second time? His instinct was to use height to his advantage, to rain fire from above, limiting the directions of their attack. It was a safer strategy but would cause them to scatter. Instead, he chose the course most likely to catch them bunched and off guard.

He charged headlong at them.

While flying was faster, he was quickly closing the distance. Frosted earth and rock gave way beneath his weight, thrown aside by the strength of his stride. Feys called out in alarm, moved and readied for his advance, halted their own. Those on the platform were suddenly frenzied, busily working to load spears and turn cranks that aimed the weapons. Magic erupted in a maelstrom of whispers. It lit swords with acrid fire, crackled blades in swirling ice. Shields bubbled forth, and arrows cried to be loosed.

Stone did his best to avoid the most damaging barbs, as he finally reached their ranks. He allowed his wings to be hit, even used them to shield his body when an arrow might have struck something vital.

"What brazen folly!" the lead fey taunted, as Stone crashed through their ranks. "You may not fear magic, but you will learn to fear fey!"

The few who had thought to strike by sword learned the folly of facing a dragon without the safety of distance. They were met with brute force and uncaring blows by claw and tail. Clinging fire followed after. Magic shields did little to protect them from such an onslaught. They were crushed aside in an instant, burned clear through in the next. They didn't even slow his momentum, as Stone leapt at the machines. One had loosed its lengthy barb, but the aim was off. It scraped the scales from the side of his right leg and nearly skewered another fey.

Arrows took him in both wings as he'd entered the fray. One caught the underside of his left arm. Another nicked an ear. Stone landed atop the leftmost platform. It wobbled beneath the strain but did not tilt.

"At this very moment," Stone called back to the lead fey and tore the weapon to pieces with great swipes of his claws, "I fear nothing!" He swiped his tail with a roar, struck through the second weapon. He shattered it to pieces, along with the fey desperately trying to aim it his way. "Tell me where my friends are!"

Stone jumped from the platform, used its height to claw an archer who'd flown too close. Arrows continued to strike his hide where he wasn't able to deflect them. Dozens sprouted from between scales, had even split two down the middle. He did as Willow had done, used an arm to swipe across and break them with ease. The barbs were still embedded in his flesh, but at least they no longer hampered movement.

"Surrender," the lead fey said through gritted teeth, "and I won't kill them. Yet." Apparently his burns were not fully healed. His movements were jerky, pained. He held his icy sword in both hands as he faced Stone. "I will not ask twice."

"Nor will you have to."

Stone surged forward and turned aside, so the sword would strike his shoulder and not his neck. It pierced straight through, past scale and muscle, embedded into bone. Its enchantment was already spreading ice toward his heart, as his mouth closed over the fey. The agent's scream was short lived, his shocked visage the last he'd make. Stone spat the upper half of the fey's body aside. With an agonized effort, he managed to pull the sword free from his shoulder. It clanged against the ground in ashen echoes.

Ten feys still remained, and they knew he couldn't fly. They loosed arrows and magic from a distance. While Stone brought three more down with fire, his wounds were becoming too extensive and too numerous to ignore. The numbing cold in his shoulder had stopped grasping for his chest, but the ache of it still pained him. It was difficult to stay afoot, let alone continue the fight.

I have no choice, he growled inwardly, calling upon anger to keep him going, willing his body to keep moving. *If I'm captured now, no amount of healing will save me. I'll have failed Crier and Glim.*

He breathed streams of raucous fire one blast after another, careful to choose those who flew within range.

Fortunately, his reach was nearly equal to theirs. It took skill to leap close enough to attack and yet breathe with enough force to break through their protective magic. He dodged what he could, blocked with wing what he could not, but the ire that fueled him was waning. He suddenly longed for his own magic to shield him as theirs had.

He glanced back at the metal platforms. Both were still held aloft by enchantment. An idea came to mind, as he blocked arrows with a wing. He turned and dashed toward one, upended it with a claw. He then gripped it by the top to hold it in place. It was effortless to turn, to use the platform as a shield. Though his strength was nearly spent, this new tactic gave him hope.

I'll use their own magic against them, he thought with a toothy grin.

There were seven feys left, and they were running out of arrows. Stone could hear every word passed between them. All were afraid, desperate to stay alive. Once talk of retreat to gather help began, he knew time had run out. He didn't have it in him to give chase, nor could he heal fast enough to deal with reinforcements. Even if he defeated these last remaining fey, there would no doubt be more to deal with in the city.

He looked back toward the massive spires and the thousands of feys flying about without a care for his existence. How would he even begin to search such a place? It was then he caught sense of another group heading out. Not just a group but a small army. His heart sank and hope dwindled. His grip on the platform began to falter. There was no point in carrying on against such odds.

The army drew closer, thumping the earth with rocky footfalls. A single fey flew among them, her wings beating a familiar flutter. And in front came light steps, the small frame of hope renewed. It was Crier and Glim, with a hundred rocklings at their backs. With all his worry and hardship, it had never occurred to Stone that they'd be coming to rescue him.

– 11 –

Stone reluctantly woke.

He'd had a good dream and was loath to leave it. He was on his side, with Crier lying against his face. The boy was gently caressing the soft hide beneath an eye. He had no idea how long he'd slept, could only vaguely recall allowing himself to pass out once he'd seen they were both safe. Glim was there too, resting behind an ear. The slight flutter of wing and steady pallor of breath meant she slept.

"I wasn't sure I could bring you back," Crier said in a hushed tone, mindful Glim was lightly snoring.

Warden magic flowed through, warming every muscle with murmured song. Wounds healed, body and wings restored, Stone felt genuinely rested. He realized Crier wasn't healing him at the moment.

He was comforting.

Stone replied, "I was thinking much the same thing, before you came to my rescue."

They were still out in the open, where Stone had fought back the feys. The boy's army stood watch in a wide circle, smaller humanlike creatures made of rocks.

They looked like precariously placed stones that could tumble at any moment. When they moved, however, it became apparent some unseen force held them together. There were others there as well, walking patches of mud and moss. Crier called them loamlings. And, of course, airlings swirled through the currents just above. He didn't sense any treelings, though, most likely because there weren't any trees to be found.

At the sound of his voice, Glim had snorted awake. She flew over to face him, smiled wide and hugged the horn on his snout.

"I'm so glad you're alright!"

Stone chuckled, nearly shaking Crier from his perch. "I'm glad to see you well, too. I was worried, to say the least. What happened in the city?"

When she let go his snout, he looked past to the twisting spires. Feys were still clouding the open spaces between, but none seemed to be gathering weapons or rallying for another attack. No more drumbeats could be heard in the chilly stillness.

"I was placed in a crystal cell." Glim pulled tight her silken wrap and shivered, from cold or the memory he couldn't say. "It seemed especially designed for me, or at least someone like me. The crystal was marked top to bottom in sigils, enchanted to give off light, even the floor and ceiling. There were no shadows to hide in, not even my own. They took my clothes," she said and looked away, cheeks reddened in shame. "They asked questions, over and over, about you and Crier, where we lived, how we survived, what we had planned to do at the great tree. They refused to let me feed or sleep, only brought me water when my voice began to fail. I didn't tell them what they wanted, though. When I refused to cooperate, they bound my hands behind my back, so I couldn't—" she stopped to clear her throat. It seemed difficult for her to speak of what had happened. "There were dozens of them, seated all around outside my cell. They just stared at me, like I wasn't one of them, while a Magister asked her questions. I'd never felt like that before, like I wasn't a real person. I was just a thing." She looked over at the boy. "If it wasn't for Crier..."

"I'm sorry it took so long," the young Warden said to her, his own voice strained with emotion. "They kept me in a half-sleep with the same drug they used to capture me."

Stone eased Crier off and stood. He lowered his head and touched the spot between his eyes tenderly against Glim.

"I'm glad you were not harmed," he told her and meant it with all his heart. She and Crier were as much family now as Willow. "And you," he said and turned toward the little Warden, "how did you escape? How are you able to maintain so many conjures?"

The boy was trying his best to hide it, but Stone could sense the toll such an endeavor was taking. His presence was wan, his beat a trifle quick. A handful of airlings to play with was nothing in comparison to the assemblage he'd created.

"Because I have to," Crier answered. In that moment, he looked older, more like the man he would become than the child he'd always been. "Without them, I would have never gotten free or found Glim. You, on the other hand," he said and laughed, "were easy to find. I heard you halfway across the city, from inside a double-walled building!"

"Yes," Stone agreed with a wry nod, "they were intent on keeping me captive. I did my best to convince them otherwise."

Crier noted the scorched and trampled earth. "I can see that." Though the fey bodies were nowhere in sight, mounds of overturned soil formed a steady line off in the distance. He'd likely had the rocklings bury them out of respect. The boy had always revered life, even if that life had meant him harm. "We should get going," he said and reached up, asking Stone to lower his neck. "I'll explain along the way. We need to reach the great tree as soon as possible."

Stone allowed him to climb up. "The egg?"

Glim nestled in beside him. "The tree itself," she said. "He thinks it holds the answer to restoring all the forests. Not just ours, but all of them at the same time."

"What about the conjures?" Stone asked and lifted off. "They won't be able to keep up."

"We need them," Crier replied into the wind caused by their speed. "Right now, they're the only thing keeping Commander Thistle from attacking."

Stone could sense the creatures follow but not in the manner he'd expected. Rather than run atop the earth, they'd somehow burrowed and tunneled after. Only the airlings were able to fly alongside.

The Commander, Crier explained, led what remained of the Conclave's military in Corrund, the city they'd just left. There were six more cities in the Hollow, each one of them larger than the last. It wouldn't take long before reinforcements rendered aid. Without the conjures to act as a visible deterrent, every agent under Thistle would follow after.

They passed over a shroomden patch with stalks as tall as any tree. From far above, their overlapping caps seemed to form another landscape. Stone thought it best to fly them safely overhead rather than risk any traps, magical or otherwise.

"Which reminds me," Stone called back, "how will we deal with the trap that caught us in the first place?"

"Leave that to me." Crier sent his airlings ahead. They

were surprisingly quick. "I was barely conscious, but I saw how to pass through without harm. I don't want to take any chances, though, so—"

A crackle of lightning erupted just ahead on either side, from two ends of a crystalline opening. The harsh sallow of their demise was like a fading spasm in air, a bittersweet breath of dying whisper. The rocky channel headed upward from there, lit by glowing crystal in pale ringing and smoky chill. Three more traps were disabled in a similar vein before they exited into night and to their old forest home.

Sense of it caught Stone with a shiver of alarm. The bite of it was in his nostrils before it touched his eyes. Sight of it gave way to panic, a fearful grip upon his chest. He knew too well the familiar blare, the orange tingle of its embrace. Worse, he knew who'd caused it and why.

The great tree was on fire.

* * *

Stone turned away and flew higher, brought them up over the treetops. His instinct was to rush toward the flames, to find a way to put them out and save the great tree. That could've been just what she wanted, to keep him distracted while she struck. He had no illusions about a direct encounter with his sister. She was the larger of them now and could easily best him. Even more frightening, she used to be the smarter of them as well. Her quick wit and patient strategy were more often than not their only reason for passing mother's tests. From the way she'd acted during his capture, some sort of madness had taken hold, had eroded her mind from her time of torture and the following years. How long had she been driven by delusions of his betrayal? How much had her unbalance affected her judgment? While this attack on the tree might appear as a slight, an insult to what he cared for, there was something of his mother in the ploy. He feared the whole of it was a scheme, one of his sister's stratagems.

He was afraid her aim was to harm Crier.

She'd bragged of her ability to stay close but out of sense. If she was near, he wanted to find her, to try and reason with her, to reclaim the sister he'd loved and lost. There had to be a way to convince her he wasn't at fault. She'd suffered a terrible ordeal, one he would've gladly changed places to spare her, but none of it had been his doing.

"The tree!" Crier gasped. "It's on fire!"

Stone had circled around, was doing all he could to find any trace of Willow. So far he'd sensed nothing, no glaring odors, no broken tree limbs. His firm resolve had begun to waver. Could the conclave have done it? Was their magic even capable of such a feat?

"I'm searching for a greater threat."

"We *need* that tree," the boy shouted and sent his airlings. "What threat could be greater?"

"My sister," Stone replied and headed toward the fire. He couldn't be completely certain she wasn't there in the forest, but neither could he risk Crier jumping off to deal with the tree on his own. "I wanted to be sure it wasn't a trap."

"Your sister?" Glim asked with tentative surprise. "I thought she was—I thought she died when you were young."

"So did I."

When they reached the great tree and hovered over its top, it became apparent the fire had been caused by a dragon. Ignited bile dripped down in heavy gobs, ran in rivulets along stony limbs and the massive trunk. Sticky flames were working their way toward the forest floor and set alight the winter dark in angry glow. The petrified wood might not have normally burned, but this was no ordinary fire.

Airlings were trying to douse the viscous flames with grayish whirls and jarring blasts, but not even chill wind could stay its course. If anything, their attempts spread the bile out in splatters. Crier had let go all his conjures but those fighting to save the tree. He called forth others in air to join, sent them scurrying to lend assistance. He seemed at a loss for what more to do.

"We need water," Glim suggested. "The nearest river is in the Hollow."

Stone said, "The snow." The ground below was nearly covered in a thin blanket of recent fall. There were icicles as well, drooping down from lower branches. "Have them gather snow and ice, apply it to the fire."

"That's brilliant!"

Crier had often spoken to Notch, though Stone didn't understand any of what the treeling said. Here, however, he merely made gestures with his hand and seemed to guide the airlings without a word. Was he able to hear their thoughts or convey his own without speaking?

They rushed to do his bidding, like animated whorls of wind. Flashing in the dark, their glowing eyes traced a path toward the snow far below. Rather than take it up in a semblance of handfuls, the airlings swirled through and accumulated the snow within their bodies. Icicles broke away one after another and joined in their roiling winds. They were a storm of conjures, growing whirlpools of ice and snow.

When the first of them rose and touched upon the fires, a billowy hiss escaped from their collision. Great tufts of discordant smoke surged outward into steam and left ashen trails in their wake. The once wood had been marred, like scars upon their surface, but no longer did it burn. When the concerted effort of numerous trips had finally doused the tree, Crier let the airlings go and slumped over in exhaustion.

"You did it," Glim congratulated. She flew over to sit behind him, to make sure he didn't fall. "You should rest now. Go ahead, close your eyes. I've got you."

"Yes," Stone agreed. "Good work. I'll take us home."

Crier said, "No, don't." If his body was as weary as his voice sounded, he was in desperate need of sleep. "Just land at the base of the tree. I'll sleep there. Please, it's important."

Stone relented and settled down before the illusory opening. He wanted them both to stay outside, however, in case they needed to leave in a hurry. He asked Glim to fetch the egg, while Crier nestled between two large roots. Stone nudged rocks over and carefully heated them to keep the boy warm. He considered searching the forest for his sister once more.

Glim returned and placed the wooden shell halves near Crier. She fastened the neck of his top, the way she'd doted on him when he was small. She then flew over to join Stone a fair distance away.

"I wish we'd brought a blanket or two." Glim landed between two of Stone's talons, pressed against him for warmth. "It'll get colder before dawn."

"I'll keep the rocks heated," Stone said and lowered himself to the ground. It wasn't safe to leave them alone. "Did they hurt him?"

She seemed surprised by the question, glanced over at Crier and shook her head.

"He's too important," she said. "Most likely they used threat of harm against us to control him. I'm glad he fought back."

"He wasn't taught to back down."

"No," she said and smiled, "I suppose not. He's more

dragon than human in that way."

Stone snorted. "I was talking about you. Dragons back down all the time. We're only fierce when we know we can win."

"I've only ever seen you retreat when someone else's life was in danger. You're plenty fierce," she added, "even when the odds are against you."

"Maybe," he conceded. He thought of the lead fey and Magister Sorrel, how they were both convinced he was something else. "Apparently, I'm not like other dragons."

"I could have told you that."

The wind was growing stronger. There was moisture in the air, a faint promise of new snow.

"Did they hurt you?" Stone asked.

Her wings twitched. "Just my pride. I thought I was stronger than that. I didn't think anything could bother me the way—" She stopped, looked up at the stars and took a moment before trying again. "I was expecting to be tortured. I'd almost rather that than the humiliation. It just reminded me of my mother, how everyone treated her when they found out she was a Shadow Walker." She wiped her cheek with the back of a hand. "It was like I was back there again, when my brother first saw me shift and turned me in to the conclave. My whole family—everyone I thought who loved me suddenly...they treated me like I wasn't one of them, like I wasn't fey. Like I was an animal, but worse. They hated me. My own father *hates* me." She tried to fight it but openly cried. "And I've never done anything wrong. All I ever wanted was for my family to love me, for who I am, to not look at me the way—how everyone did when I was in that cell."

"I'm sorry," was all he could think to say. He wished he could do more to comfort her but considered what she really needed was just a caring ear to listen.

They sat together in silence as the hours began to

pass. Stone did his best to keep her warm, to hold her close with a gentle touch. Eventually, she fell asleep in his claw. He warmed the rocks around Crier two more times before morning. He'd foregone any sleep to keep a wary eye out for his sister. She may have been watching, but he saw no sign that she was.

Wherever she is, Stone thought with an aching sigh, as morning song broke through the trees in scattered beams of golden warmth, *I hope she's alright.*

- 12 -

Where Crier slept, renewal had spread.

The roots beside him had softened once more to living wood, reached out into earth sprouting vine and winter flowers. At his back, the bark had lost its stony visage and was home to a new layer of moss. Sap dripped from a knot into an eddy of amber sweetness, pooled and fell again onto a patch of budding grass. Thorny blossoms, twisted brambles, fresh shoots and the surge of pristine air; it looked as if Spring had forced awake the Autumn slumber.

The boy yawned and stretched. When he saw Stone watching, waiting patiently for him to wake, Crier smiled and got to his feet.

"I know what happened," he said and indicated the trees, "the forests, dragons, all of it."

Stone placed Glim in the spot where Crier had slept. Though she wouldn't complain, he could sense she was weak from hunger. She most likely hadn't fed since they were captured. He quietly nodded toward the trail, that they should move away before speaking. Once they'd gone far enough so as not to disturb Glim, he motioned for the boy to continue.

"There is a single tree," Crier explained, "a massive, unbelievably large tree, whose roots touch upon all other trees in every forest. It's called the World Tree," he said, as if he could see it in his mind, "and without it all the world will die."

"The trees then," Stone said, "feys didn't cause them to petrify? Something happened to this tree instead?"

"Both. This is what happens when they feed too much, when they don't give the trees time to recover." He touched a hand to a nearby trunk, and its bark began to brown with renewed life. "Wardens are protectors and emissaries of the World Tree. We keep it safe, replenish the trees and help the forests stay clean and healthy."

Stone grunted. "And when the Wardens were killed, there was no one to undo the damage caused by the feys overfeeding."

"There's a balance," Crier agreed, "one we need to put right. Things are worse than we thought, though. I don't even know where to start."

"Where all things start," Stone said and nudged the boy playfully with his snout, "at the beginning. Whatever needs doing, we'll do it together."

Crier nodded, and though he smiled he looked troubled beyond his years.

"There have always been three," he said, "Wardens I mean, but now I'm the only one. In the past, when one died, another was born to take their place." He shivered and hugged his arms to his chest, looked down at his feet as he spoke. "I'm the last. I'm the only human left."

"I am truly sorry," Stone told him with sincerity, "for the part my kind have played. I was just a hatchling at the time. I still feel responsible." An idea came to mind. "The feys have magic. Couldn't one of them become a Warden?"

"From what I've been told," he replied, "it was human magic that created the World Tree. It was meant to save a dying world in a time when the trees were failing. It grew sentient, had a magic all its own. When human magic began to fade, the tree created Wardens to keep it safe."

"Well, then it can create more," Stone suggested. "We just need to find it."

The boy's voice took on a new tone of utter sadness, as if he'd witnessed its death firsthand.

"The World Tree is no more," he said. "Dragons didn't hunt every last human to extinction. They burned the tree down to its core and starved everyone to death. Crops refused to grow, disease spread, forests withered, entire species of animals and insects died. The very air is slowly dwindling. Soon there will be none left. Nothing will survive."

How could this have happened? Stone thought with sudden anger. According to Sorrel, his own father had been the cause of it all. *How could he have been so shortsighted?*

"I wish dragons had never been born," Stone said with vehemence. "Why Wardens saw fit to create us is beyond me."

"You were meant to protect us," Crier said. "When a Warden died, a new one was born. They needed time to grow, to master their ability, to learn to be a Warden. Since there were only three at any time, they were weak during this period. There was an occasion when all three had passed in a short span. Wars broke out. There was famine, pestilence. The water and air became sick. Tens of thousands, across all races, died while those Wardens grew."

Stone nearly growled in frustration. So much of the world's history was unknown to him. His mother had taught them nothing but lies. Why had she hated them so much?

"And once they'd grown, their answer was dragons?" Stone huffed. "A better option would have been more than three Wardens."

"The tree cannot sustain more than three," Crier said and shrugged. "Each is gifted a unique ability, and there are only three to gift."

"You're still here," Stone pointed out, "and you have more than one ability. If the tree is gone, how are you a Warden?"

"The last High Warden had a staff, a splinter of the World Tree. It's alive. The tree's spirit was housed within its trunk, inside an amber crystal called the Spirit Stone. It too was destroyed by dragonfire, but five pieces of it were already kept in the Wardens' collection of magical artifacts. If we can find just one of those Life Stones and touch it to the staff, a new World Tree can be planted inside the old one."

"How will we do that?" Stone asked in exasperation. It seemed an insurmountable feat. "The only Warden artifact we know of is the egg I found you in."

Crier said, "I don't think finding a Life Stone will be near as difficult as acquiring the staff. It was last seen with the dragon who led the assault on the World Tree. His name is Eboncall."

It felt as if Stone's world had shrunken in to a pit of darkness, an endless well in his middle fueled by guilt and disappointment.

"I know he's your father." Crier tried to comfort him, put a hand to his snout. "It's not entirely his fault. The Wardens were betrayed by one of their own. It was he who killed the other two and gave the staff to Eboncall. With it, your father was able to ignore the maker's bond. He could harm the World Tree, the Wardens, ignore the rules imposed on him and every other dragon by the very magic that had created them."

"For what?" Stone shook his head at the futility of it all. "To set fire to the world? To spend the rest of eternity in hunger?"

"To be free," the young Warden answered plainly, with compassion and understanding. "They didn't ask to be created and were enslaved to a purpose they neither chose nor wanted. They asked to be set free and were denied. They tried to fight to be free and discovered they couldn't. The magic that gave them life had imprisoned them as well. They were governed by a set of rules, like an instinct they couldn't ignore."

"What of this maker's bond now?" Stone asked. "Can you use it to force my father to give us the staff? And what of the third Warden? If he killed the other two, where is he now?"

Glim was starting to wake. Their voices had grown loud. Crier looked back toward the great tree and shook his head.

"Jacoben hasn't been seen since he gave the staff to Eboncall. The great tree doesn't know why he betrayed them, but he and his sister were never seen again."

Sister? Stone's heart began to pound, though he didn't know why. Did he feel a sudden kinship with this Warden? An understanding as to why someone could do such a thing? *What might I do to save my own sister?* he wondered, and a world of terrible thoughts soon followed.

"As for the bond," Crier went on, "it's still there, but whatever commands dragons were given died with the Wardens who had spoken them. I could give new ones, but I won't. I will never use a dragon that way. Besides," he added, "Eboncall is immune, so long as he has the staff."

Stone scoffed. "How will we get it from him, then? Ask nicely and hope—"

He sensed the spear coming toward them before any trace of the krag. This one was different, barbed like a blossom at both ends before the lance. And it was accompanied with the whisper of drummed song and echoed chants.

The dragon hunter had found them.

* * *

The veiled whispers of fey magic rang out through Stone's mind, as Willow appeared in air just behind. She knocked the spear aside and rolled to all fours. Snow and earth erupted around the force of her bulk, each claw gouging a trail to full stop. The bone spear had struck and passed through a heartwood, splintered its bole into the flaring creak of collapse. As its branches shattered against the frozen ground, the dragon hunter held out a hand.

While this spear had been carried with all the speed and aim of enchantment, it didn't vanish into wisps of smoke like the last. It was embedded in the face of large rock. The cracks it had caused lengthened, until debris ruptured outward. The shaped bone sought to return with as much deadly haste as it was thrown.

Though she sensed it break free, it caught Willow off guard. She twisted to one side, avoided the brunt of its impact. The pointed blade at either end missed her thigh by a scale, but the bristled spikes at their bases tore through. Blood splattered across the frost and steamed in protest. The hunter caught his spear with little effort.

Willow roared in pained anger.

Stone was quick to grab Crier and run toward the great tree. Glim was fully awake, eyes wide and shocked still. The hunter stood his ground, assured and unafraid. He still wore the same clothing of fashioned dragon hide and scale across his groin and chest, but he now carried a shield as well. The symbols across his flesh glowed a chorus of maroons.

Fire raged with such fury, its heat distorted the air between. Willow had loosed her breath with a deafening sulfur cry. It shook snow from the trees. It rattled the very earth. And through it all the hunter stood, shield raised against the blast. Bolstered by his magic, it blackened but wouldn't yield. Molten bile fell from its scales, dripped to hissing puddles at his feet. When it seemed her breath was about to give, he plunged his spear into the ground, pulled a pouch from his belt and threw a cloud of bitter dark into her face. Air caught in her throat, but the fire persisted. She hacked and sneezed, fiery globules thrown wide. No amount of shaking or snorting would clear the substance from her snout.

Stone had turned and protectively covered Glim and Crier with his body. He was torn between the instinct to carry them from danger and rush to face it with his sister, no matter the cost. His love hadn't diminished in the least. She was still the other half of his heart, the only half of him that mattered. He'd rather die than live without her again.

Rocklings began to claw their way up at the hunter's feet. He pulled the spear free, reached for his belt with the other hand and fluidly threw a knife. It sped toward Crier, a high keened whistle as it cut the air. Stone stood in front, blocked it with both wings. Blue light flared across the blade, glowed bright like a heated ember. It sliced clean through his body and struck Crier in the middle. Rocks tumbled to the hunter's feet and remained still.

The boy made a sound like he'd been punched. He looked down in disbelief, confused by the handle sticking out from his stomach. He reached for it with shaking hands but seemed afraid, as if touching it would make it real.

"Stay out of this, little Warden," the krag said in a deep voice unused to the language, "or your next wound will be much more severe."

The pain was irrelevant, hadn't even registered in his mind before Stone spun and eased Crier to his knees. Glim was not so calm. Her face reddened with sudden outrage. Fists balled, she became shadow, a seething roil of directed storm. Her shade raced across the distance, darkening between trees and lengthening out from a fissure of fallen rockling. Shadow blade in hand, she slashed up across his abdomen as she rose. The umbral edge could not sever the dragon scales below his belt but parted flesh between the markings with ease. Though it wasn't a deep cut, skin on either side of the injury curled in ashen flakes. Tufts of shadow flame briefly emanated from the wound.

Where a lesser warrior would have reached to stem the flow of a sudden gash, the hunter fell back a step into a sturdier stance. Rather than block her next attack, he chose to dodge it instead.

"I have faced your kind before," he warned, in that odd manner of speech. He turned his upper body aside to avoid another strike but didn't move or back away. He reached again for his belt. "You will not be my last."

Glim screamed her frustration, more flailing with her blade than choosing the right opening. She'd cut him two more times, but the wounds were superficial. When he pulled a small glass phial from his belt, he reached out with it in hand as she stabbed through his bicep. A cacophony of light exploded from his palm. The blast threw Glim to her back. A phosphorescent liquid coated her front, forced her to shift from out of shadow.

"You are fey?" the hunter asked in genuine surprise.

Stone held Crier up, did his best to keep a steady voice

as he spoke.

"You have to heal it," he told the boy. "Don't take the blade out until you're ready. Understand? Crier! Look at me. I know it hurts. You can do this. Call the magic, like we practiced. See it in your mind. That warmth, that fire, it's yours. It's in you. Call it up, temper it with cold and pull the knife out."

Crier nodded along, lips trembling, fighting to keep his eyes focused. Warden magic began to murmur, the growing rise of a hushed call to the crescendo of a torrid whisper. The healing flames took shape in his hand, the crisp blue of ancient ice. He snatched the blade free with the other and pressed the fire to his wound. His body seemed to fill with healing light, so much so that a glimmer escaped his mouth as he gasped.

Across the way, Willow had had enough with fits of coughing and violent sneezes. She plunged her snout into the snow, cleansed it with the melt. She whipped about without warning, her tail careening through the air. It struck through half a dozen trees before barely missing its intended target. The hunter tumbled away at the last moment but couldn't fully avoid the strike. It took him at the shoulder. He landed in a heap and slid beneath a falling tree. Quick reflexes allowed him to scramble out of its way, and the fractured tree joined the others in a blinding crash of stony branches.

She limped after without delay, a towering visage of toothy nightmare. Claws smashed down with each step, crushing tree trunks like glass. The hunter rolled back and up, extending his spear to its fullest length and swiping out as he got to both feet. Willow lunged forward for a bite and caught the lance beneath her chin. Scale and maw parted into a bloodied mess. She was beyond any pain, lost to a building frenzy. One claw swipe after another sent up chunks of earth and rock. She slammed her tail down behind her with enough force to shake the ground. Though the hunter nearly lost his footing, he had dodged every attack. He bled from numerous cuts caused by debris but had avoided her massive talons. Willow reared, called up bile and lurched ahead to set it free. The hunter's spear went out in tandem and caught her upward through the snout.

Viscous fire splashed from both sides of her mouth, poured from the wounds on top and below. Liquid flame and a crimson torrent, it washed over the hunter's arms. He shouted in agony, as the fire ravaged his flesh. His markings glowed anew. Her breath hurt him, but he wouldn't burn. His magic kept him whole but not free of the pain.

He pulled the spear out and rolled aside. As Willow reeled and roared, the krag moved with all speed to put distance between them. He neither needed strength nor sufficient balance to hazard a deadly throw. The weapon was enchanted. Its magic did all the work. He turned and threw without missing a pace, continued to run. Though she deflected with a wing, it caught her once more on the return. Both her hind legs injured, it became difficult to move. Another throw went through a wing and glanced her neck on its way back.

Willow stumbled from the rapid blood loss. Glim had frantically used dirt to scrub the burning from her front. Crier was mended but lacked the strength to stand. He struggled for the magic to conjure any help. Stone saw his sister falter, and his heart missed a beat.

No, he swore, a lethal promise put to action. *Not again.*

He was moving before thought, with no plan or solid purpose but to save all that had ever mattered. Despite injury he flew, just above the ground. Claws carried him when wings couldn't. He charged headlong in, dodged the spear when it came and leapt for all his worth. Stone missed with his left claw but caught him in the right. Though he seethed, there wasn't time. He knew it was coming.

Stone turned and held his claw out.

The spear plummeted through, impaled the hunter to his claw. Blood and fury became one, a shaking tremor of reckless gain.

"Why!" Stone demanded, unlit spittle dripping in open threat. "You wear us like trophy, use our bones as a weapon! Why?" he asked again in a drawn out growl.

The krag labored to move and was squeezed for his efforts. His markings blazed beneath the assault but couldn't stop the bones from breaking. Barely able to draw breath, the dragon hunter finally spoke.

"I have...no choice!"

He'll never stop, Stone realized. He was a prisoner, a slave like dragons. Whatever magic protected or helped him hunt also bound him in unseen chains. *Another form of maker's bond.*

Stone loosed the full might of his breath upon the krag. Markings flared, screams rang out, but in the end the magic failed. Fire freed him from his bond. It burned clean the enchantment, ate away the flesh beneath. The strength of it was so intense, so devoid of restraint that it carried on through. It took half of Stone's claw before he let it abate.

Exhausted, shaken by pain and the surge of ire leaving his blood, Stone hobbled to his sister and knelt beside her. She'd died once again, her lifeblood across the snow. He waited this time, refused to hear any other voice. And when the heartbeat came, he nearly cried, out of joy, out of relief, out of knowing she'd return. Her eyes fluttered open and met his.

"You stayed," she said and saw the ruin of his claw. "You fought for me? Risked your life?"

"I would do anything," he replied, "*anything* for you."

Willow smiled, and for a moment they were together again. But that joy quickly turned into anger. She shoved him away, got to her feet as if burned and scrambled away. Barely footsteps from where he sat, she vanished in a cry of whisper. No more prints, no lingered scent, she was just gone in a single instant.

– 13 –

Stone fell to his stomach and lay still.

He'd come so close to reaching her. It was there, in her eyes, for that all too brief a moment. Like a glimpse of their childhood, of all he'd taken for granted, memory and reality had coincided. It was a bitter joy. For a short while, she'd loved him again or at least remembered why she had in the first place. Given time, she might come to see the truth. All he could do until then was hope.

They both came to him at the same time, weary and shaken, worried for one another. Friends at either side, each a hand out to comfort Stone, they stayed together in quiet solace. When snow began to fall, a flake tickled Crier's nose. He laughed despite the solemnity of their situation. He rubbed away the moisture, tried to reclaim his thoughtful poise. This caused Glim to laugh. The two shared an uneasy happiness, merely glad to be alive and still in each other's company.

"We should head back home," Stone said at last. He felt healed enough to fly and didn't care to lie around, gathering snow upon his backside. "We'll figure out what to do from there. It's not safe to stay here."

Crier said, "We need to go the other way, to the east. Eboncall's lair is beyond the veil, near the coastline."

"Those lands" Glim pointed out, "belong to the sprigs and redcaps. Even flying over them is dangerous. They don't like outsiders, or each other, for that matter."

"We don't have a choice." Crier got to his feet and wiped the snow from his breeches. "We need the staff to plant a new World Tree."

"A what?" Glim asked. "Did I miss a conversation?" She flew over to collect the wooden egg halves. "You know how I feel about being left out."

Stone stood and stretched his wings. There was still much for them to discuss and no telling when the feys would strike next. He didn't feel much like talking, though. What he wanted was to go search for Willow. But how? She'd vanished from sense right before him. She'd *used* magic. Fey magic, to be precise. It hadn't made her merely invisible. She'd completely disappeared, as if no longer there. How could he hope to find her against such a magic?

"You're worried about her," Crier said to Stone, "your sister. I could tell from the horns and her colorings. You look a lot alike."

He lowered his neck for them to climb.

"She's been through a great deal," Stone said. "I don't know how to reach her, to help her see past the delusion. It's...troubling."

Glim secured the shell pieces with silken cord, as Crier settled in. By the knit of her brow and flaxen scent of unease, there was something bothering her as well.

"She used conclave magic," Glim said and strapped herself behind a spine ridge, "the same used by scouts and assassins. How did she do that? I understand she might be unusual, like you, unafraid of magic." Glim shook her head, trying to come to grips with an idea contrary to all she knew or had been taught. "But I've never heard of a dragon using magic. It goes against their nature."

"Eboncall used the staff," Crier pointed out. "It's not exactly the same, but maybe she's doing something similar."

"Like an artifact?" Stone asked. He glanced back at the Warden circlet fit snugly to his wing horn.

"Right." Crier held on tighter as they lifted off, called out into the growing wind. "It didn't look like she had time to cast a spell. She's either very good or using some sort of enchantment."

"That makes sense," Glim reluctantly agreed, "but doesn't explain how she came by it. Is she working with the conclave? Did she kill an agent and take theirs?"

More importantly, Stone thought as he carried them out of the forest, *was she still following?* He wanted to believe she was nearby, that she hadn't given up trying to see the truth of what had happened. *Why else would she have tried to save me? Twice, now.* He refused to think she'd watched him all this time just to torture him. *No. She holds out hope. As I do.*

"Wait!" Crier shouted and leaned forward. He pulled on the silken cords around Stone's neck out of habit, which elicited a none-too-friendly look his way. "Can we go back to the hunter's camp? All those dragons. Some of them might still be alive."

"No."

"I can help them," the boy pleaded. "It's cruel to leave them chained and dying like that."

Glim put a hand to his shoulder in understanding, but her voice was firm.

"It's too dangerous," she said, "for all of us."

Stone didn't slow or change direction. "The world is better off without dragons."

"You don't believe that," Crier accused, though it

seemed he was trying to convince himself more than his friend.

"I do," Stone said evenly. "Look at all the destruction we've wrought, all the ruin we've brought. What would the world look like right now if dragons had never been created?"

"That wasn't you!" Crier shouted. "And it wasn't them." He crossed his arms and sat back. "Well, I don't believe it. I don't think an entire species should be held accountable for something only a handful did decades ago. You're a good person. And so is your sister. If you think we're all better off without you...Well, you're wrong."

Is it enough? he wondered. *Could I ever do enough good to justify our existence? Even if we manage to restore the World Tree, bring back life to all the forests, how long will it be before dragons ruin it all again?* He growled and shook his head. *Are there others like me, who think and feel the same way?* He'd certainly never met any. *Does that mean they don't exist? Do they deserve the benefit of doubt? Does Willow?*

Though he knew he'd regret the decision, he turned toward the hunter's camp. It'd been a gruesome scene when last they saw it, but perhaps some of them yet lived.

"I suppose it wouldn't hurt to look."

Crier smiled and hugged Stone's neck. It felt good to make him happy, to see the same promise in others as he did—if only for a moment. Stone knew how dangerous his kind was. He had no intention of allowing his friends to be hurt. If any dragons were still alive, if Crier could still save them, Stone would make sure they caused no harm once they were healed.

Glim remained quiet as they flew. She either chose not to argue, or Crier had convinced her as well. She trusted Stone to keep them safe, if not in words then in action. They'd done their parts to raise Crier. They didn't always agree, but their intentions had never wavered.

Wind carried sense of it beyond the hills before it came into sight. Its ruddy grasp poisoned the air, a foul miasma of dank decay. The pool of congealed blood at its center was overwhelming in its cry. The dulled echo of blighted flesh that joined the chorus swam in the bitter browns and rancid grays of dead meat. Through sense of it all, the closer they drew, not a single beat of life could be heard. Slashed and broken against the rocks, chained down or pinned, none had been meant to survive. Lures for the trap, their only purpose had been to draw more in. Dying smoke lilted up from the hunter's campfire, wisps of ash within the snowfall. Even its few remaining embers would soon be gone.

"Anything?" Cried asked, hopeful.

"Not anymore."

Glim leaned over for a better look. "Should we land? Maybe we're not close enough to tell for sure."

"I'm sure," Stone replied. After some consideration, he looked back to meet Crier's disappointment. "I'm sorry we couldn't help them."

Crier looked away and nodded. "Let's go home."

They went the rest of the way in silence, though not entirely by choice. The snowstorm had intensified into a drone of azure gale and swirls of ice. There was too much risk in trying to rise above the thunder. The clouds had grown into an impenetrable mass. So they endured the blinding hail, fought against the winds. Glim and Crier huddled close, used Stone to shield them from the worst. Between the grating flashes, the terrible gusts and sleet in his face, Stone was forced to close his eyes to pass through the worst.

The tempest only lessened as they left it behind, and within hours their mountain home came into sense. It was a mixture of emotion that rose up within his chest.

Stone was glad to be back among familiar surroundings, near the lair they'd made together as a family. But there was something amiss, a foreign prickle he couldn't place. There was dread in the air, the sort that warned to stay away. It gave a shiver down his spine, one the others felt as well.

"What is it?" Crier asked.

Glim was alarmed. "Stone?"

"Something's wrong," he said and carried them into the tunnel. "I've never sensed anything like it."

Though the trees were all intact, half their forest had been ravaged. Most of the bushes and wild plants were now blackened to ashen twigs. Swathes of flowers and grass had wilted, stems browned and fallen over. It was a different sort of devastation. It reeked of magic, not fire. Its whispers were still alive, still slithering between the trees.

They were darkness come to life, tens of them within the shrouding. Their whispers worked as one, like a tribe of lightless hunger. Each stood at the sound of Stone's claws touching ground. They had arms and legs, a head but no face. They looked as Glim did when she shifted. Blades in hand, they came forward, and with them came the dread.

* * *

"They live in the shadow of the Wall," his mother said in an ominous tone, eyes beaming in the delight of their fear, "in a darkness permeated by magic. Forever cursed, they hide from the sun or suffer its touch on pain of death. They draw life from the plants, until the ground becomes cold, barren and empty. If ever you should come across them, flee for the light, for they fight without mercy and cannot be killed."

Shadwens, Stone thought, his mind stricken with a horror instilled by his mother's stories. He looked back toward the tunnel. Night was falling. Would moonlight be enough? *We must flee!*

Glim had already loosened her bindings and flew down to meet them.

"No!" Stone warned.

Notch was there, scrabbling at a leg with trembling branches. Crier slipped down to comfort his friend.

"Glim!" Stone hissed. "Come back! We must leave," he told the boy, struggling with the instinct to turn and leave them both behind. "Get back on!"

Glim stood in front, waiting. She watched them with interest, unafraid as they approached. In her mind, they must have seemed like fellow Shadow Walkers, kindred spirits she so desperately wanted to connect with. They were crouched, cautious and avoided the reflected glow of cavern crystals on the ice. Hollow whispers carried with them, phantom voices in the breeze. They were not the murmurings of magic. Blades disappeared into their hands. They seemed more curious than aggressive, as each surrounded Glim.

"They do look fey," Crier said in response to Notch's twittering. Why were the others not as alarmed? Shadow Walkers or not, these creatures were dangerous! "Though I didn't think they fed on plants. Are any of the trees damaged?"

"They are not feys." Stone spread out all four claws to balance his weight, readied to strike or draw breath at a moment's notice. "They're shadwens."

"Just wait," Glim told them calmly, watching each of the intruders with a careless fascination.

One reached out and touched her shoulder. Without warning, Glim shifted, as if the touch had caused it. The others followed suit, moved in close to offer greeting. A rise of murmurs went up, and one of them was Glim's. In turn, each embraced her. It was as if she were a lost child found at last. They didn't appear to mean her any harm and talked together for some time.

Stone relaxed and eased his stance.

"They seem to know her," Crier said. He gave Stone a friendly pat on the leg then moved forward with Notch at his side. "Are you going to introduce us?"

The visitors gathered behind Glim, as she turned to face her friends and shifted back.

"They recognized me," she said, on the edge of joyful tears, "what I am. They're just like me."

"You're a shadwen?" Stone asked, confused.

He still fought with his sense of them, the fear their presence inspired. It was nothing like Glim when she walked in shadow. He wasn't afraid of magic. What was it about them then that put him so on edge?

"They are fey," Crier said. Whatever sense he'd used to draw the conclusion was beyond even Stone's. A sort of Warden's insight? "I'm certain of it."

"I don't have all the answers yet," Glim said.

There was something to her tone, a trepidation and hesitance that spoke more than her words.

She's leaving.

Stone wanted to growl, to shout at her to stay. It didn't matter how alike they were in nature. They were strangers. They couldn't be trusted. She didn't know any one of them any more than she knew the conclave. It was foolish and reckless to even think of leaving. Little more than a short conversation and she was ready to change everything in her life? To risk losing it? How could she even consider throwing away all their years together?

He caught her watching his reaction. She knew him better than he knew himself, saw his wordless temper growing. It fluttered her heart with sadness and cooled his ire in an instant.

Why was he suddenly so angry with her? She wasn't abandoning them. She'd been searching for something like this her entire life, other feys who understood, who saw her as a person. She'd spent her life as an outsider to her own people, hated by blood kin, hunted for what she was. These creatures were offering her a chance to belong, to feel accepted without judgement, to be a part of a larger whole. Who was he to stand in the way of the one thing that might make her truly happy? He felt guilty for even thinking she should let that slip away. She'd become like a sister. As much as he wanted to, as much as he'd miss her, he couldn't ask Glim to ignore such an unexpected opportunity.

"They want you to go with them," Crier said with a downcast nod. He stepped closer and hugged her. "To find others like you...it's incredible. This is something you've wanted for as long as I can remember. I—I will miss you dearly." He sniffled and hugged her tighter, as if afraid he'd never hold her again. "You will come back, though?"

When she let go, her brow was crinkled in surprise.

"I—of course, I will! How could you even ask?" She looked to them both with the emotion born of a lifetime together. "I'll miss you, too, and I will *always* come back. To both of you," she said to Stone. He saw in her glance that she was asking for his approval. No, not approval. His understanding. Stone gave a low bow of his head in acceptance. She clutched both hands to her chest and smiled in silent thanks. "They know my grandfather," she explained. "Not my fey grandfather, but—"

"The one who truly sired you," Stone offered. "He was a shadwen."

It began to make sense. But how could they be fey if they were always shifted? Had his mother lied yet again, or were her stories about them true? Had they been cursed, driven from their homeland and forced to live in fear of the light? Had they been transformed by magic and become dark feys? How did a shadwen and a fey even mate?

"Not me," Glim reasoned, "my mother. She was a Shadow Walker, too. I inherited her gift." They began to murmur, like voices haunting a distant tunnel. "I don't understand everything they're saying. They speak in an older dialect. Some of the words aren't even gaelish. At least none I've ever learned."

"But you have to go," Crier said. He reached out and held her hand.

Glim gave it a squeeze with a pleased look. "He's still alive. My *grandfather*." She spoke as if she could hardly believe it. "They say they can take me to him, but we have to leave now. There's more danger for them than moonlight in traveling at night." Glim shook her head with a little laugh. "They call me Light Walker, like it's a blessing."

She's so happy, Stone thought, ashamed it should grieve him. *Why can't I just be—*

"I'm glad for you," Crier said. "Go see your family. I hope you find everything you're searching for. Hopefully, we'll be back with the staff by the time you return."

"Or else," Stone said in a grim tone, "your other family will come looking."

Glim expressed her gratitude. "I'm counting on it."

Their goodbyes were short but sweet. The shadwens had been growing more impatient, insisting they needed to be on their way before the moon hit its apex. When they left together up the tunnel, Glim was in shadow. Though it pained them, though they'd miss her, Stone and Crier did their best to be happy for her.

"Should we have offered to go?" Crier asked, still watching the tunnel as if she might come back.

"I don't know that we would've been welcome where they're headed." Stone turned so that the Warden shells faced the boy. "Untie these, please. We'll rest for tonight. Gather everything you think you'll need for the trip. We'll leave in the morning."

Notch's leaves shuddered in protest.

"We have an extremely important task," Crier said to his little friend and set down the wooden pieces. "We may be gone for a while. Perhaps it's time for you to do what we discussed, go to your favorite spot and put down roots." He fussed over the treeling's leaves. "You'll make a marvelous tree. I'm sure of it."

Branches fluttered in complaint.

"What?" Crier nearly laughed. "No! She won't eat you. She'll be gone for a while as well. I promise you'll be safe."

Stone huffed and turned toward the tunnel. It had been a long day with enough turmoil to last a lifetime. Though his wounds had healed, he still ached. His body and mind were tired. He wanted to be strong, for both Crier and Glim, to put forth a brave face.

But the hurting in his heart would not abate.

– 14 –

Stone's sleep had been fitful. He'd spent most of the night in restless worry, anxious about facing his father, torn between their task and chasing after Glim. He had faith in her judgment, that she'd made the right decision for her. He had faith in her ability, as a warrior and a survivor, to fight free if that judgment had been in error. Neither, however, could alleviate his misgivings. If the shadwens betrayed her, if they hurt her...

He'd tried more than once to put the thought from his mind. Fantasizing revenge for imagined slights had done little to help him rest. What he should have been concerned with was how he and Crier intended to wrest the staff from his father. Eboncall was the oldest and largest of dragons, the one who'd caused it all. He wasn't going to simply hand it over.

The light of a campfire flickered by Crier's tree. He should've been sleeping but had spent most of the night studying the shells. The egg's magic had been spent. If there was anything to be learned from the broken halves, Stone doubted it would be useful in the coming fight. He sighed at the azure coloring of Crier through the tree.

That's how he's always been, Stone thought and put his claws beneath him to stand, *never focused on the fight until it's already upon him.*

Despite years of teaching, to hunt and fight, to spot danger at a distance, the boy had always seen conflict as an occasion to be avoided. Such an outlook was perilous for a dragon, not so much for a Warden content to chew fruit. Unfortunately, contention has a way of finding the unprepared.

And there was no way to avoid conflict when walking into a dragon's lair.

"Are you ready to go?" Stone approached the tree and peeked inside. Crier was holding one of the shell halves with his eyes closed. "Did you sleep at all?" When the boy didn't respond, Stone moved his head inside and asked, "Is everything alright?"

He gave a short burst of air.

Startled awake, Crier dropped the shaped wood. It fell over and wobbled near his lap. He rubbed at tired eyes and gave a weak smile by way of apology. With a yawn, he got wearily to his feet and wiped the dirt from his backside. Something was amiss, from his somber mood to distinct lack of cheerful conversation. Either the reality of Glim being gone had struck home, or the boy had learned something troubling during the night.

The fire was nearly out. Rather than feed it more twigs and fallen branches, which were scarce, Stone heated its surrounding stones. Besides, it wouldn't do to waste resources when they were leaving so soon. Lighting a fire was rare, as cutting down one of his trees was out of the question. Crier would normally have used a crystal to see by within the tree, but their glow faded in time with the setting sun. He must not have wanted to bother Stone during the night.

Or was it something else? Stone wondered. It almost

seemed like the boy was trying to avoid meeting his eyes. Crier left to gather fruit and vegetables for the journey. *Is he hiding something?*

"Are you worried about what we'll face?"

"I haven't given it much thought," the boy replied and chose pieces that had already fallen. It didn't take long to fill his satchel. "I miss Glim. I know she's hardly been gone a single night, but—I guess I'm just thinking of all the nights and days without her still ahead."

"She will return," Stone offered by way of comfort. Not that the notion in any way eased his own desire to have her back. "The world has been without its Tree for some time. We could put off our endeavor, go after Glim instead."

Crier frowned and looked at Stone as if he'd offered to burn the world again.

"No," he said and tied closed the leather satchel. "It's too important, and we're running out of time. We can't let this go on any longer."

Is he upset with me? Once Crier had gathered a traveling pack, Stone lowered his neck for the boy to climb. *Does he blame me for letting Glim go? She's not mine to command. Neither of us had the right to make her stay.*

Once Crier had settled in, Stone asked if he needed to say goodbye to the treeling.

"Notch put down roots last night," Crier said, "in the center of the garden. We already said our farewells. He's no longer a treeling. He doesn't need me to sustain him anymore."

Stone moved toward the tunnel.

"Does that bother you?" he asked and pushed off into a bitter breeze. "It's understandable if you're upset."

"I'm not upset," Crier replied a bit defensively. "Let's just go. I don't really want to talk right now."

The sunlight felt good across his back, a continuous pitch of budding warmth to fight back the winter winds. There were storm clouds in the distance all around them, impenetrable layers of darkening gray, but their own sky was clear for a few more hours. Snow covered the hills and mountaintops, had even blued to ice in large patches in the ravines. No patterns or prints marred the snow in a beckoning call, nor were there trails of colored scent ringing out as they flew. Whatever life persisted in the colds below, it chose to stay within the relative safety of underground.

They flew east for some time before passing between their first forest home and where the dragon hunter had set his trap. Stone hadn't sensed any others of his kind since they left. While he imagined some would soon move in to mark their claims, a large part of him wished there were no others to take their place. The time for dragons had passed. They'd shown what they had to offer, and the world was poorer for it.

Crier had at least rested before they reached past the mountain range that marked new lands beyond. He was loosely strapped in behind a spine ridge, hugged it close for warmth while wrapped in a blanket. He woke as they breached the plains, gasped as they soared downward into an unfamiliar place.

The flatlands and hillocks offered little in way of life, but for the groves of mushroom and few copses of stony tree. Snow covered them both in a winter bedding of blinding white, muffled all but their passing and brash wind in their ears. No grass or brush poked through nor had it likely for many years. While the land should have been too far east for shadwens, it hadn't seemed to stop the feys from devastating all the trees.

The mushrooms here were very different from those growing in the Hollow. Their stalks were shorter and far wider, so much so that a race of people had made their homes within the trunks. The caps were thick and twice as broad as their support but didn't crowd the space between. They grew far enough apart to allow sunlight to strike the snow, though the fast approaching town had little of it on its ground. The snow had been pushed out into a large circular drift. It no doubt protected those who'd built it from the wind. Smoke billowed upward from a number of controlled fires. Whoever these people were, they all seemed hard at work.

Stone turned to go around the settlement. He didn't want to risk flying over, as there were hundreds of the stout creatures. There was no telling if they had similar contraptions to the feys, metal machines made for the sole purpose of killing a dragon in air. He thought he'd given enough distance to not appear as a threat. The three who came up after must have disagreed.

They flew atop large insect-like instruments, though not nearly a quarter the size of Stone. Comprised mostly of iron and copper, there were bands of animal hide that rotated and caused four silken wings to beat quite fast. Their whirring and metal clanks flashed out a dissonant clamor. Dark belches of acrid smoke occasionally burst from out the back. Had the wind shifted it might have obscured vision for the occupant, but all three seemed to be wearing leather bound glass across their eyes.

The redcaps Glim spoke of? Stone surmised. *She didn't mention they could fly.*

The people were somewhat akin to the mushrooms they made a home in. They were shorter than a human, even a fey for that matter, but much wider and thick of limb. Each had a spot atop their heads where the bone was exposed, a spatter of bright crimson amidst hair tied into a length. The coloring nearly matched their stained lips, teeth and beards. They had long, pointed noses and short, tapered ears. Their skin was darkened by the sun, smeared with dirt and ash. The fumes their machines spewed suffused their scent into a din of browns.

"Who *are* they?" Crier asked in equal amazement.

Stone had reared to a halt at the sight of them. He was in a bit of shock, still gauging what threat they posed. Could their machines cause harm as well as fly? The lead redcap carried a wooden length tipped with a crystal, while the other two's were made of hollowed iron. Staves weren't much of a weapon at this height, but each held them as if they were.

"I've never come across anything like it." Stone beat his wings to stay in air, far more slowly than the other three. "The feys had large weapons that fired spears like a bow. They could float across the ground, but they were nothing like this."

The lead redcap held up his staff and halted beyond the range of breath. The other two came to a stop just behind. He seemed much older, his hair grayed from its once black and face wrinkled by many years. He stood within the machine and brandished his staff, thrusting it outward in warning. The crystal at its head came alight with a yellow glow that flashed with intensity each time he held it out. Its whisper was new to Stone, like a deep resonance of echo within a cavern or a tunnel. It was a drawn out calling, like a chorus beneath the earth.

"He has magic," Stone cautioned and considered if they should turn back toward the range. It would take a considerable amount of time, but they could wait until night and fly even further around the settlement. "If we stay any longer they might attack."

Crier leaned to one side for a better look.

"I don't think it does anything but light that crystal," he said. "He's not actually using magic, the way I would. It seems like the magic is in the staff, and he's activating it. Like how your sister disappeared."

Stone gave it some thought. Could they be trying to scare him off, because dragons are supposed to be afraid of magic? He called out to the redcaps, loud enough that they could hear him across the distance.

"Why do you block our path?"

The elder redcap looked confused, held the staff out toward them with more fervor. The intensity of its light remained the same. He nervously glanced back at the other two. One shrugged, stood, and leveled his metal staff at Stone. It didn't appear to have any magic.

"We just want to pass," Stone told them. Could it be they spoke a different language? "Can you understand my words?" To Crier, he said, "I don't think they're used to dragons who stop to talk. Care to give it a try?"

The boy stood and shouted, "Hello!" When none of them responded, he called out a word Stone had never heard before. "Calen!" He'd emphasized the second half. "Oendo!"

He cried out two more words before Stone realized he was speaking different languages. Where had he learned so many tongues? Exactly how much knowledge had he gained from his conversation with the great tree? Or was this one of the three gifts granted to him as a Warden?

The redcap put down his staff, and its glow faded from the crystal. He cupped a hand to his mouth and shouted out to Crier.

"I understood the dragon," he said in a curious way of speaking. It wasn't that he was unused to the words, like the krag had been, but there were lilts to the way he spoke. "I just never met one that didn't shat itself at the sight of magic. I'm a bit flabbergasted to see a human as well, let alone one riding a dragon. Are you a Warden then?"

"I am. My name is Crier, and this is Stone. We don't

mean you any harm. We just need to pass through."

"I'm Durden," the redcap said. He indicated the other two and added, "This is Forlen, and that's Korklen. Care to land and have a word? We've a problem you might could help with, and we'd be forever in your debt."

"Alright," Crier answered. "Just lead the way."

Stone had thought it a ruse, that once the redcaps descended, he and Crier would fly past. Why else would the boy agree to land, when they were perfectly capable of speaking in air? But no, as soon as Stone moved to fly onward toward their destination in the east, Crier began pulling on those damn reins.

"Where are you going?" he asked with incredulity, as if Stone was somehow the one oblivious to their plan. "We *just* agreed to land."

"You were serious?" Stone grunted and came to a stop. "We can't trust these people. Glim said as much before we left. They're dangerous!"

"They could have attacked us and didn't," Crier said.

Stone quickly replied, "If you wait for your enemies to strike first, you'll always be at a disadvantage."

"If you're always waiting to be attacked," the boy said with pity, "then everyone you meet becomes an enemy. We can't live like that and build a better world."

"I don't like it."

"I know you don't." Crier patted him on the neck. "That's why I have you to keep to me safe. These people need our help. The very least we can do is hear what they have to say."

The very least we could do is leave without a word, Stone grumbled to himself and began their descent.

The redcaps had landed beside a river. It was a good distance from the settlement, so he didn't have to worry about arrows. If their encounter was a trap or some sort of betrayal, Stone could easily burn the three and their machines. He and Crier would be gone before anyone from the town could react.

Sense of the river struck him, like a physical attack on his innards. Its foul grip shook him with a blackened shriek, a fetid scrape across the tongue. Its polluted waters were so vile he nearly retched. Dark masses of rotted pulp floated across its top, foamed and bubbled the surface in a miasma of noise. Whatever caused such contamination had long ago died. The unmistakable feel of death rang all throughout its waters.

"What is that?" Crier asked with a hand over his nose and mouth.

"Rot," Stone answered as they touched ground near the redcaps. "Something's fouled the water upstream."

The three had left behind their flying instruments and approached on foot. Each had raised the glass above their eyes, which revealed an ashen outline of clean skin. Durden removed his gloves and waved. He caught sight of Crier's dismay. He took in a long, deep breath, then coughed it back out.

"Takes a bit of getting used to," the old redcap said with a wry grin, "but there's nothing to be done for it but try and clean it as best we can." He pointed toward the settlement. "The community's in rough shape. Most of us are sick, the bairns worst of all. The goats and callies do well enough, but it's getting harder to feed them. We eat mushrooms for the most part." He reached into a pocket a pulled one out, handed it to Crier. "But it's getting to be too much for them as well. Our structures are failing, our magic all but gone."

Crier bit into the mushroom. It oozed a red liquid upon his lips and teeth. He seemed to enjoy it somewhat and finished the rest. If that was all the redcaps ate, it was no wonder their mouths and beards were stained. Crier pulled a golden apple from his satchel and gave it in return. He knelt to examine the river, while Durden made short work of the gift.

"Bit too sweet for my taste," the redcap admitted, bits of apple in his beard, "but a damn far sight more filling than a shroom. What do you think, can you help us?"

"I can try." Crier hadn't touched the water but paid close attention to the detritus floating past. "I could cleanse a separate water supply, like a barrel maybe, but the only way to purify the river is to find what's causing this."

Korklen blew out a breath he'd been holding, while Forlen sucked at his teeth. It appeared they'd already come to the same conclusion and had little success in dealing with it.

"What is it?" Stone asked. He'd been keeping a close eye on the other redcaps in town. A large group of them had gathered by the snowbank to watch. "You've already tried?"

"Aye," Durden said and scratched at his chin.

Forlen crossed his arms. "Fat lot of good it did. Three days, and all we managed was to dull every blade we could find."

"I don't understand." Crier picked up a handful of snow and poked at it with a finger. "What exactly is it dirtying the river?"

Durden opened his mouth to explain but seemed to struggle for the words.

"It's probably best we just show you."

– 15 –

Stone led the way south along the river, pushing aside snow with his bulk. The last fall hadn't been thick, but it gave the redcaps a bit of trouble. They stood two heads shorter than Crier, with legs half as long. Durden had mentioned they were more accustomed to riding goats than tromping across the hillsides on foot. With the sickness having taken its toll, there were few still strong enough to carry a bag of coal, let alone a full grown dwarf. That was another thing he'd pointed out to Stone as they walked. Apparently *redcap* was a derogatory term only "worm-diddling feys" used. Durden and his people were *dwarves*, kuergan to be exact—which meant dwarf of the hills. Much like how feys weren't limited to living in the Hollow, dwarves had many clans across Eralle.

The pollution grew worse the further along they went, spread to the surrounding snow in putrid slush. There was a heat to it, steaming off the surface, bubbling over rocks, though the water remained an intermittent blue. It was only the debris, in stringy lengths of crimson and orange bray, that carried with it any warmth. The river flowed in stark contrast to the purity of fresh snow. When

Crier had asked if the dwarves tried to melt any for water, Durden told them they had. The river, however, went right through Oasthold. There was no avoiding its effect on the soil.

"I didn't think I'd ever see another Warden," Durden said after a while. It might've been easier to fly them all ahead, but Crier had insisted on walking to survey the land. Forlen and Korklen were just behind and speaking quietly together. "I was certain humans had been wiped out. We all sent trackers, even those of us who've never gotten along. We knew what would happen without a Warden to tend the Tree." He gave Crier a sidelong look of sorrow and apology. "There was nothing left. Every report was the same. From Highgarde to Norvale, Sky's End to Surcrest, every human city had been razed to the foundations. Never have I seen anything like it."

"You were there?" Crier asked.

"Norvale, aye. I was a pathfinder for many years before my brother fell ill." Durden grabbed up a handful of snow, crunched it between his fingers and let the bits fall away. "I'm chieftain now. There's nothing I wouldn't give to have him back."

"What about the cities?" There was excitement in his voice, despite the horrendous loss. Crier was often all too desperate to learn anything of his people. "There must be something left in the ruins, buried libraries or—"

"There's nothing," Durden replied. "I know it's hard to imagine an entire city of stone and metal reduced to ash, but—surely you've seen him use his breath," he said and indicated Stone. "Nothing and no one can withstand it. It burns clean through until there's nothing left, and it keeps burning long after the dragon's moved on. Tell me, can you control all the dragons or just this one?"

Stone turned and leveled an irritated glare toward the old dwarf.

"No one controls me."

He steamed the air with a huff before turning back to continue walking.

"He's my friend," Crier explained. "Stone found me when I was a baby and raised me to be a Warden."

It was Durden's turn to huff, though his was more in disbelief than any anger.

"Are you sure he's a dragon then?" He held up both hands to Stone to show he didn't mean any harm by the question. "I mean, you *do* know dragons hate Wardens don't you? That's how this whole mess started in the first place."

Crier stated firmly, "Stone is different. There's no one like him. He didn't just raise me to be a Warden. He's going to help me plant a new World Tree."

"Well," Durden said, "it's as wild a tale as ever I've heard, and I wouldn't believe it if I hadn't seen with my own eyes. If there's anything we can do to help, you need but ask."

Stone looked back over a shoulder as he walked, appraising the three dwarves. From what he'd gathered of feys, only the males grew hair on their faces. Yet, every dwarf he'd seen in town had a beard.

"How do you mate?" he asked the chieftain plainly. When Durden stammered for a reply, either embarrassed or unsure of the question, Stone elaborated. "If dwarves are all male, how do you sire offspring?"

Forlen and Korklen laughed.

"We're not all men," Durden said. His cheeks had brightened beneath its layer of soot. "We've women like anyone else."

Crier seemed to be looking for a delicate way to phrase the question, when Stone merely asked, "How can you tell?"

The two dwarves in back laughed even harder.

"Bosoms aside," Durden answered, mindful he was talking with strangers to his culture, "they're softer than men. Their eyes, lips, cheeks and beards...they're softer, less rugged. And they're leaner than we are. Generally. That's how you can you tell at a glance."

There was a rocky hillock up ahead with an opening barred by vines and fallen trees. While the river flowed past it on one side, it looked as if water fed into it from the hill's crevice.

Stone had been considering the dwarves as a people since they left. They were very different from feys, from their appearance to mannerisms, clothing to way of living and even in the sound of their words.

"Why is *redcap* offensive?" he asked.

Durden grumbled. "It's a sort of play on words the feys think is clever. The morells, err, mushrooms we live in used to have bright red caps. Much brighter than the red of our skulls but close enough for a taunt." Durden spat a gob onto the snow. "Calling us redcap was a way of saying we've mushrooms for brains."

Whispers reached his sense, like the rustling of wind through leaves. It was similar to the Warden magic, a feel of coaxing, reaching out. This song was grounded in earth, in the tangles of roots stretching forward, in the branches intertwined, in the leaves layered one atop another.

"Not all that clever."

"The morells," Crier began with hesitation, "what happened to their color?"

"Faded with the Tree," Durden said, though Stone felt it was more a guess than a definitive answer. "The sickness hasn't helped. All grayed and wilting," he said and shook his head. "Soon we'll be out of our homes and forced to live in the mountains or underground like our cousins."

"Pssh!" Forlen scoffed, while Korklen said, "Bah!"

"We'll see what we can do about that," Crier said in consolation. He nodded toward the hillock. "Is that it?"

"It is," Durden said. "Hopefully your friend here has better luck getting through than we did."

Stone had stopped a tail length away to study the strange configuration of tree and vine overgrown across the entrance. He thumped three different spots, but their echoes revealed nothing beneath the rocks and frozen earth. There was a tunnel ahead, beyond the growth in their way. The trees and vines were alive, warm with leaf and fully rooted. The magic coming off them was proof enough that neither had occurred naturally. The tarry substance and pulpy lengths that filtered past the rocks and barrier were another matter. They led down a scored path right to the river.

"They're alive," Crier said, was more surprised than curious as he stepped forward for a closer look.

Durden stayed behind with the other two.

"About the only damn thing that will grow out here," he said, "apart from spores and weeds. It doesn't take a Thaumaturge to feel the magic coming off that barricade, either."

"For days," Forlen said, "we chopped at that thing. Whatever marks we made closed over and healed like they were never there."

"Watch for thorns," Durden warned as Crier drew close. "They sprout when you get too near, thick as your hand."

"Does it burn?" Stone asked the dwarves.

Korklen replied, "We tried pitch and torches. Caused a bit of smoke but nary else. We thought to block off the river but realized it wouldn't matter. This entire area," he said with a wave of his arm, "beneath the snow is black with its poison."

"We considered digging," Forlen added, "or blasting

our way through the rocks."

"But with magic," Durden finished for him, "there's just no telling what would happen if we broke through. More trees could sprout up to block our path, or the hill itself could come down on our heads. I've sent letters to Horven, our High Chieftain, asking for help. With luck, he might send us a Diviner or a Thaumaturge." He didn't look hopeful. "We've had no word back for months."

Crier reached a hand out to one of the trees, as if he intended to speak with it. The resulting magic was sharp, like the piercing white of two rocks struck together. A wide thorn sprouted from the bark, just beneath his palm. It was nearly as big as a dragon scale. He snatched his hand away in time but did not look deterred. Rather than touch the tree, he put a finger to the thorn.

Stone growled. He didn't like reckless gambles and would've chosen to loose his breath instead. There was magic at work here, and it didn't belong to Wardens. No amount of talking was going to break through.

And I doubt normal breath will do.

"It's a dryad," Crier said, eyes closed. After a moment of trying, "He won't talk to me. I can't get anything else from the tree but *go away*."

"Step back," Stone told him. "Let me ask."

Stone had already set about calming his mind. There was no danger nearby. He could afford to leave himself vulnerable while his body worked as a conduit.

Crier opened his eyes and frowned. He knew there was no other way. Either these trees burned, or the land would suffer further. Nostrils flared in defeat, he trudged away to stand with the dwarves.

Stone took position before the entrance. He drew in one, long final intake of air and loosed his breath with the full fury of his creation. The stream of ignited bile burned blue-orange to red-white as its temperature grew in strength. It was difficult to maintain a prolonged blast in this manner, whereas a usual burst was meant to merely scorch. His mother had called it the heart of fire. It was a state of mind that induced rapid bile production. The longer it burned, the more he breathed, the hotter it would grow. She'd said it was the only time a dragon could call upon the magic that had given them life.

Nothing could survive the heart of fire.

Bark blackened and wilted beneath its touch, curled in and retreated into char that sparkled blue. Vines came apart in withered browns, their leaves to ashen powder. Thorns sprouted and cried out beneath the pops and crackles of moisture dying away in an instant. Embers blossomed within the trunks, set aglow the entire length. Not only did the branches fade to cinders beneath the flow, the cavern entrance itself began to melt. Rocks softened to a bitter glow and dripped in silent plea. Like a gaping wound in the hillock, the cavern opening spread before them. It bled fiery stone amidst the roil of ebbing magic. The tunnel beyond widened to orange glowing ripples of molten slag.

"Gods below," Durden murmured, and there was fear in his voice.

The few remaining trees split, fell over in the tumult. They continued to burn and crackle long after Stone had ceased his breath. The bile pooled like flaming magma, mixed with liquid rock and carried embers to the river. Stone collapsed, filling his lungs with deep draws and struggled to steady the incessant pounding in his head. He'd only used the heart of fire twice before, once when his mother had taught them...and again when she'd cast him from her lair.

"Stone!" Crier ran to his side, put a hand to his neck. "Are you alright?"

"I'll be fine," he said in reassurance. "I just need a

moment to catch my breath."

The cavern entrance continued to burn.

All three dwarves helped to put it out with snow, but it was a long and tedious process. While they'd managed to fill the area with a misty billow of steam, it seemed the fires only went out once the bile had been spent. Outside the entrance and well into the cavern, the ground had been scored with smoothed pits of melted rock.

"I've seen the aftermath before," Durden said and wiped sweat from his brow, "but never fire as that. I don't think anyone's ever seen a dragon breathe like that and live to tell of it. Your breath—it's magic."

Forlen stood just inside the snowbank caused by the backlash of hot air. The blackened earth behind them for two wingspans was without snow. Muddied from the melt, it showed plainly the devastation caused by poison leaving the hillock. Korklen used a rock to dig at the mud and see just how deep the corruption went. The hole was as deep as his arm before he found unspoiled earth. They both still looked shaken, too afraid to go near Stone.

"I'm fine now," Stone said to Crier and stood. He was tempted to head upstream and wash the muck from his underside. The matter before them was more pressing, though. "Shall we head inside?"

"Let me go in first?" Crier asked. "I think the dryad might receive a Warden a little better than the dragon that burned his trees."

Durden harrumphed. "For all he knows," the dwarf said and followed behind the boy, "you told him to do it."

The other two declined to join them.

What would have been impossible for Stone to pass had become only a tight fit. He hoped there was no need to suddenly flee back outside. Turning around wasn't an option.

An emerald light came from up ahead, a warm glow

like beryl sunrise. It carried through the tunnel breeze in stark contrast to the brackish sludge beneath their feet. The smell was awful and echoed off the walls. It felt as if Stone was being barraged with its stench on all sides.

"For the love of—" Durden began and gagged. "Smells like a troll ate eggs for a week straight, shat itself to death and caught fire in the process."

Crier was further ahead, a hand over his mouth and nose. There was no avoiding the muck, so he focused instead on the magic. Its whispers were unrelenting, a hoarse chorus of weary pleading. It was strained, losing strength. Whatever spellwork the dryad plied, it would eventually kill him.

Stone sensed it before the others and stopped in silent awe. It was nearly as tall as he and wide enough to crawl inside. The hollowed opening was alight with dryad magic, bathed its walls in the green of early spring. Its striations were a form of spellwork, a continuous flow of enchanted language no eye could see. Its whispers had long since quieted, but he knew the moment it touched his sense. The giant root wasn't merely extraordinary in appearance.

It belonged to the World Tree.

– 16 –

Stone sensed the dryad within the outpouring, at the center of all its whispers. They'd grown frantic, forceful, fighting in vain to assault the root. Ashen black, devoid of life, the wood warped only a little within the wailing but wouldn't break. The magic was akin to Crier's but more raw and unfettered. Its indelicate touch seemed born of exhaustion and frustration. Along the inside of the root, it failed to breach the wood. Instead, it became poison, dripped down into a pool that ran along and out the cavern.

He's trying to heal the root, Stone realized, *but the Tree's spirit is gone. Nothing can bring it back. Forcing something dead to heal is causing the corruption.*

The dryad was inside the root. He stood much taller than Crier, though terribly thin. Leaves grew from his head within the grass of his hair. He was bare but for the flowers about his waist. Lengths of bark ran the outer edge of both shoulders and thighs. His skin was earthen dark and emerald eyes aglow within the magic. Shaking, crouched, struggling to draw breath and persist, he watched Crier approach.

"I understand," the boy said. Stone had stopped to listen, could not go any further. "But it's too late. You must know that by now."

"My trees are gone," the dryad said. Though his voice was raspy, parched, it elicited memories of wind through full boughs of colored leaves. It was the voice of a pure spring, feeding the soil and thirsty roots. "I have nothing left." He looked at the dead wood, saddened by its refusal to live again. "I have to save the Tree. Without it, I am lost. No reason to go on."

"Restoring the Tree is a Warden's task." Crier put a hand to the dryad's, to speak with more than words. "I promise to put things right, but you must stop. You're hurting the land and its people."

The dryad had its eyes closed as they spoke. He pulled his hand away and glared at Durden.

"People!" he said with a derisive grunt. "Monsters."

Durden crossed his arms and scowled. Crier frowned and shook his head at the dwarf in warning to be quiet.

"They think," Crier said, "they feel, they love and they hurt. They're people, just like you and me."

The dryad gave pause. After a moment, he pulled a hand away from the root. The magic wavered. He held his head in hand and began to tremble.

"Without a tree to tend," the dryad said, voice broken and weary.

Crier reached out once more to touch his hand.

"Let me show you," he said. "I've created a forest. It won't be easy to get to, but it flourishes to the west. You can be its caretaker."

The magic ceased, as the dryad's eyes went wide at whatever vision he was seeing. He took hold of Crier with both hands and smiled.

"I can make it," he said with certainty. "I'll—I'll travel beneath the mountains. Are you sure?" he asked Crier, a firm grip with both hands. There was an edge of madness to his eyes, a desperate spark of hope. "Can you make it live again?"

Crier nodded and looked back to Stone.

"We can."

"I'm going to rest now," the dryad said, wiping tears of joy from his weary face. He lay down within the root. "It's been too long." A final smile to Crier, he added, "May we see each other in dream."

"Sleep well," Crier said.

Before turning to leave, Crier put a tentative hand to the root. It was apparent he'd hoped to learn something from the Tree. His crestfallen look held disappointment enough for them both. Stone sighed and began the slow, tedious walk backward out the cavern. Once outside, Crier plunged both hands into the icy water and did his best to cleanse the river.

"It will take time," he said, once he'd done all he felt he could. "The land will recover on its own."

"You made a forest?" Durden asked with skepticism. He looked as if he'd been weighing the question in his mind before asking. "From nothing?"

Crier replied, "It's one of the Warden gifts."

Forlen and Korklen had already started back to make plans for a celebration. Durden remained with Crier, a troubling thought upon his brow.

"You have them all, don't you? The Warden abilities," he said. "High, Low and Balance." Before Crier could ask how he knew, Durden added, "That means you're the last of them. They really are gone. Humans, I mean. An entire people, just gone." He rubbed at his face while grappling with the notion. "I never imagined it could happen, not in my life or any other."

Stone looked toward the east.

"All we can do now," he said, "is move forward."

Crier agreed. "We need to work together, to fix what's been done and make sure it doesn't happen again. If we can't restore the Tree, it won't be long before all of us are lost."

"And after you're gone?"

They'd begun heading back to Oasthold. Durden walked beside Crier, while Stone took the lead. Stone had offered to carry them, but the dwarf asked for this time to talk. Once they'd returned to town, any hope for conversation would be lost beneath the revelry.

"I honestly don't know," Crier replied. "Wardens were created by the Tree. Once we plant another, hopefully it will be able to find a solution before—before I'm gone."

"One foot at a time," Durden said.

Stone said, "A good a plan as any."

Durden took off a metal chain from about his neck. He handed it to Crier. There was a medallion attached to one of the iron links. Upon its copper surface was a crest painted in red and white. It was a mushroom cap and a cog, beneath an emblazoned letter K.

"Your way forward will be clear," the dwarf chieftain said, "at least from kuergans. The sprigs will be another matter. If any dwarf stands in your way, you show them that medallion. They'll let you pass or deal with me."

Crier slipped the necklace over his head.

"I'm honored," he told Durden. "Thank you."

They returned to Oasthold not long after, with the setting of winter sun. Crier accompanied Durden into town to meet the other dwarves. Stone remained outside the noise and crowd of celebration. He cleared an area far enough away that he could keep sense of Crier and not be blinded by dwarven music. The metal clinks, the blare of pipes and incessant drumbeats went on without end. Bonfires were raised, and cheers became a common occurrence once they'd all started drinking fermented mushrooms. The feast as well was an assortment of cooked mushrooms, moss and lichens. No goats were made a meal of, as their milk was more precious than the temporary meat. One was offered to Stone as a gift. He declined the generous gesture. It would've done little to ease his hunger, and the dwarves needed it far more than he.

After many hours of festivity, meeting most if not all the dwarves and their boisterous offspring, Crier bid them a goodnight and returned to Stone. The dragon had cleared a circle with breath and tail, lined it with large rocks and warmed them in preparation. He rested in the center, curled against the wind. Though the music was less insistent, the merriment went on. Crier had trudged a path through snow and into the clearing. He took a blanket from his travel pack.

"They're so different from the feys," he said and lay against Stone's middle. Stone opened an eye but said nothing. "You're thinking of her, too."

Always, Stone thought but said, "It's hard not to."

Crier bundled up within his blanket, put a cheek to Stone's softer underside.

"What do you think it's like," he asked, "whatever world the shadwens live in?"

"Magic and darkness."

"She's alright, though," Crier said, voice weary from the day. "I mean, of course she is. She's with family."

Stone curled around him even closer.

"So they said."

* * *

Stone woke of a sudden in the wan silver of early morn. His heart pounded in alert but body frozen in fear. All sense had erupted at her appearance. One instant he was lost to dream and in the next abruptly stirred beneath the shadow of his sister. Willow emerged amidst a shout a fey whispers. Tendrils of smoky black clung to her frame for but a moment then faded into the rising steam of fevered hide within the cold. Her maw was close enough to press against Crier. She remained still before him, studying, as if gauging his worth. Not what value he held to the world but for what he meant to Stone.

Crier woke to the warm breath touching his cheek and hair. He opened a weary eye her way but didn't startle. Instead he shifted to face her and gauged her in turn. He slowly reached out a hand, held it waiting for her. Willow nudged him with her snout, allowed him to place his palm against her.

Stone's mind was racing with fears, the same ones that held him fast. He was afraid if he moved, even in the slightest, his sister would disappear—or worse, she'd hurt Crier. Her eyes were closed, lost to emotion, as if she cherished the boy's touch. Stone thought to speak, to say anything that might convince her to stay. His jaw had scarcely moved when her eyes opened with wild panic.

She snatched Crier by the arm and disappeared.

No! Stone was up in an instant, snapping at empty whispers. He flung his tail wide, roared for her return. *No! Willow, please, no.*

He snuffled the air, thumped his tail, wracked his sense, but they were gone. All that remained were fading murmurs in the memory of their passing.

"Willow!" he shouted, searched about in a frantic state. There was no trace of either of them in the wind. "Crier! Please come back!"

Anger surged within him, steamed the cold from off his hide. He clenched a shaking foreclaw, eager to strike at anything substantial. Though he knew it didn't serve him to be angry, he had nothing else to hold onto. He was helpless against her magic.

She won't leave, he tried to convince himself. *She's been with us the whole time. She's always been near, hidden by that damn magic. Why take him, though? To hurt him? No. To torture me. Why now?* Stone roared and swiped at the snow with his tail. *Why now!*

What was he to do? There was no following what he couldn't sense. Was there a point to going on? He had no hope alone against his father. Even if he could somehow get the staff, what then? He had no idea what a Life Stone looked like, let alone where to find one. Nor did he know where the World Tree was. How was he to plant a new one within the old if he couldn't find it? The thought of returning for Glim occurred. She might not be able to help find Willow or Crier, but she could at least help him get the staff.

Is that my plan, then? Keep going without Crier? He roared again and clawed the earth. Breathing heavy, still furious with helpless frustration, he looked to the east. *I only know his lair is within the mountain range. How will I find him without Crier?*

"What happened?" Durden asked. He remained a safe distance away, if such a thing could be said to exist when dealing with a dragon. Other dwarves had been awakened but watched from even further away. "Where's the boy?"

Stone faced the chieftain and struggled to regain his calm, to slow his breath and think logically—the way Willow used to do.

"My sister," Stone explained. "She took him."

"How?" Durden asked, confused. "How does anything sneak up on a dragon?"

The urge to scream rose within him again. Fresh snow began to fall. Flakes sizzled into gray as they fell upon him.

"She can vanish and appear at will. Once she's gone, I

can't sense her any longer."

Durden whistled. "She has a Spirit Ring. That's fey magic. Only assassins dare wear them, seeing as they already have a, err, strange relationship with death." At Stone's puzzled look, he explained, "The ring transports the wearer to the Spirit Realm. They can see our world but can't interact with it until taking off the ring again. They become more than invisible. Like a spirit, they're still here but somewhere else at the same time."

There was something more he wasn't saying. A look of concern marred his brow, just as memory haunted his eyes.

"There's more," Stone prodded.

"The spirit realm. It drives the living mad," he said in a tone that seemed to say he'd experienced it firsthand, "and eventually kills them."

Crier, Stone thought with overwhelming concern.

"How long?" he asked the dwarf. "How long can he stay there before it's too late?"

Durden held out both hands as if to say there was no way to be certain.

"It depends on the person," he replied, "their will and strength of character. I worked with a scout when I went to Norvale, saw one of those assassins use her ring. I've seen all sorts of magic in my time, but to willingly go to the land of the dead—that takes a special kind of crazy." He cleared his throat in quick apology. "From what I was told, it was safe to wear for an hour or two, but that time lessened the more one might wear it. After that," he said and shrugged, "the wearer's life starts to fade, drained by the other spirits who are desperate to return here. The madness comes first. It could take days or years, but they *will* eventually die."

There's still time then. Willow has been using the ring for years. Crier is strong. He can withstand it until I find him.

"Is there a cure?" Stone asked. "For the madness." A plan had already begun to form in the back of his mind. "And does every assassin wear one of these rings?"

"I already know what you're thinking," Durden said and shook his head. "There's no cure, and you'll never be the same." He considered for a moment, pulling at his beard. "Do you want my advice?"

Stone grumbled. What he wanted was to be away, to be *doing* something other than talk.

"Yes."

"Ask yourself what the boy would want." Durden pulled tighter at the fur along the neck of his cloak. The snow was falling harder. "This task you were both set to. It seemed pressing. Like all our lives depended on it, that it'd better be done sooner than later."

Stone looked east once more.

"It is."

"I don't know what your sister's up to," Durden said, "and I can see you want to find her. There's no easy way to do that. He's a capable sort of fellow. Perhaps you should trust he can look after himself and continue on without him."

"Without him?" Stone scoffed. "I can't. What needs doing...I can't do without him."

"I'll go with you. Crikes, give the word," he said with a fierce chuckle, "and every one of us will go with you. It's that important."

Would that matter? he wondered. *Even with their machines, they'd all be slaughtered. I can't ask them to do that.*

"I appreciate the offer," Stone said. It truly did make him feel better, as if he wasn't all alone. "It wouldn't help where I'm going. There is something you could do," he added, thinking ahead with a hopeful thought. "If I do somehow manage to get the staff, I'm going to need a Life Stone. Crier said there were five. Can you find me one?"

"That's a Warden artifact," the dwarf said. His brow crinkled, and he scratched at a cheek. "I don't know if I can do it, but I'll sure as shite try. I'll go to Horven myself and cuff his ears to make him listen. He's ignored me for too damned long as it is."

"Thank you," Stone said sincerely.

Before Stone left to continue east, Durden told him the best route to avoid other settlements. Without the boy, Stone wouldn't likely be given the chance to explain his presence. The sprigs could be avoided, if he flew high enough over them and didn't land. He'd need to pace himself. Once he reached their marshes, there'd be no rest until he made it to the mountain range.

Then he could begin the search for his father.

- 17 -

Stone traveled for three days across snow covered hills and plains before coming into sense of the salt marsh. He'd avoided three of the five kuergan clans along the way and easily flew out of range of the other two before they could give chase. He'd flown over copses of petrified trees, small mushroom forests, winding rivers and dwindling streams, only stopping to rest at night for a few hours. He was surprised at the lack of dragons but even more so at the lack of prey. What little time he'd spent hunting along the way had earned him nothing. The skies were bare, the earth barren and the waters carried naught but empty promise. Creatures of magic, dragons could never starve. All other life on Eralle was not as fortunate.

The world truly is dying, he'd thought and suffered the hunger pangs. Those aches had become as much a part of his existence as drawing breath.

He'd questioned his decision time and again, mostly during the hours he should've been asleep. In air, he could lose himself to the cerulean pale of gusting winds, let it carry him as the melody filled his mind. It was only in the quiet moments at night, when sense failed to steal his thoughts, that the weight of loss came crashing down. His emotions varied from the rage of seething anger to the despair of helpless frustration and the hope of trusting in his friends, in their abilities and a fervent desire for their safe return.

It'd been so long since he was alone, he'd forgotten how terrible the quiet could become. His mother would've told him he'd grown soft, that he deserved to go hungry for not honing his skills with every day. Only the strong were allowed to survive. The weak were meant to suffer in hunger. They were already dead inside, meals for the taking.

Stone growled at the old memories and landed to rest before heading in. The marsh was unlike anything he'd seen before. There was a briny haze to its rhythms, a lilt of greens and browns within the mud. For as far as he could sense, the entire area was flooded. Salt water from beyond the mountains covered the land by a talon length or more. Stalks pushed up past the surface, into the chilled mist. No trees or mushrooms grew, but the water was thick with growth. A layer of murky beryl foamed across its top. It was difficult to imagine what sort of animals lived within it, let alone an entire people.

He couldn't sense the mountain range through the clouds at this distance. Rather than risk growing too weary while crossing the dangerous waters, Stone chose to rest until nightfall. With no other dragons to worry about, the sprigs were his only concern. He didn't need light to travel by and hoped to hide from them within the dark.

When night came, he took to air. He flew up into the bitter gray of budding storm clouds and biting cold. What currents swept through were brash against his scales and filled with particles of ice. A thin layer began to form across his back and down his legs. Quick spurts of fire to fly through left him warmed for a short while.

It wasn't long before the first came into sense. While Durden had warned they were deadly, he didn't elaborate as to how. Stone had assumed they were like the feys or dwarves, bipedal creatures that used weapons—possibly even magic. What he didn't expect was to be bombarded by balls of slime covered nettles while flying through the clouds.

Stone could barely sense the sprigs, massive mounds of living mud and marshland growth. Dozens of them lumbered through the water, calling out into the cold in echoed brays of booming yellow. Regardless of how they'd tracked his presence, their attacks were frightfully adept. From what he could gather as he dodged, the missiles were thrown by hand. No magic sounded out beneath the wind and whistling arcs. Stone was forced to ascend out of their reach. With begrudging respect, he climbed above the clouds. Their volleys fell short and soon faded into the distance.

It was difficult to fly at such a height. The air was thinner, colder and sapped the strength from his wings. By the time morning came, Stone could sense the range ahead, but it offered little comfort. The mountains were still many hours away. His endurance was waning, muscles burning in protest, lungs straining against the cold. He couldn't risk flying lower, let alone landing for rest. The sprigs were everywhere. Each time he eased off, another volley ensued.

Stone forced himself to endure, knew rest was ahead if he could hold out long enough to reach it. Each hour passed painfully slow. Where it was a struggle just to breathe, it was an all-out battle to beat his wings. He let the current carry him when he could, but his bulk was not meant for gliding. There was nothing to be done for it but suffer through or surrender.

He focused on his father, on the one blame could be squarely shouldered. Anger had always been a useful motivator in Stone's life. It fueled him, gave him strength and enabled him to persist. His growls and grunts of fire renewed his ebbing vigor. It propelled him another hour, when the land began to change. The waters lessened and disappeared at the base of the mountains. Snowy rocks called out their welcome as muddied lands fell far behind.

Stone more stumbled than landed when he touched upon a ledge. Scales scraped and rocks tumbled as he clawed to a stop. Wings slammed against either side of a crevice. Bruised but not broken, he slid beneath an overhang. Ice and snow fell, partially closed off the niche. Curled against a rugged wall, halfway up the mountain, he fell unconscious and began to heal.

* * *

Stone woke as the last light of winter day lost its glow to the horizon. Wind howled in silver blue across the mountain face. He pushed through the snow and ice that had entombed him while he slept. Through it all, the colors in his ears, the sounds over his tongue, scent of his father warned with a heady terror born of time. It was old, far older than anything else he'd ever encountered. There was power in its musk, a strength that dared not be challenged by one so small. It was faint only in that the marking was not recent. It stretched far to the north and south, spread its touch from base to peak. Stone began to realize his father hadn't merely marked a lair.

Ebonclaw had laid claim to the entire range.

It took more courage than effort to find it. A few peaks to the north, high up the tallest mountain, deep in the heart of its rock. The entrance was clawed wide, a natural crack torn to a tunnel. Fire and brute strength had done the rest. The cavern beyond was massive, a true testament to determination. Water flowed in from the melt of perpetual ice at the cap, while heat rose up from cracks at the base of each wall. It was as if the molten heart beneath the mountain spread its glow up to warm the hollow. Nothing grew here but numbing cold and the flickered shadow of a monster.

Ebonclaw lay curled within the warmth of a heated basin at the center of the lair. His size made Stone look like a child, was even larger than Willow. The amount of molts, the sheer number of kills it would've taken to grow so large was more than staggering—it was terrifying. He stood no chance against his father in a confrontation, healing or no. There was simply no overcoming such a disparity in physical strength.

His foreclaw was nearly as large as Stone, with thick talons that could gouge through a mountain. The horns upon his head were serrated on the outer edge, with smaller spurs at their base sprouting outward. His spine barbs were similar to Stone's but longer, flared out and curled back into hooks. His tail plates were edged, had bladed scales that reached down to further protect the underside. His stature, his power, Ebon was everything Stone one day might become.

"I know you're awake," Stone said.

An eye opened and lit the ice in reflected blues.

"It's you," Ebon intoned in a deep rumble, as if his body were a cavern of its own. His chuckle shook ice from the rock above. "You have some nerve coming here, showing yourself to me. Our deal is done. My vow no longer bars me from doing you harm."

Our deal? Stone thought. *Is he mad like Willow?*

"We've never met. I came here because the world is dying. I need your help to put it right."

Ebon raised his head to look at Stone. The ensuing

laugh was not at all what he'd expected.

Stone's heart raced with fear. It was one thing to see such a massive, deadly creature at rest. To see him rise to full height…it sent a frightful chill along Stone's spine.

"You don't remember," Ebon said. His laughter had died, but its echo still haunted. "How interesting. Does that mean I could have killed you straight away? Not that it matters now." Ebon gave an almost wistful sigh. He lowered his head toward Stone and asked, "What is it you want? Why risk your life now, after all these years?"

It took everything Stone had, all the will he could muster, not to crumble beneath that gaze. It felt as if he were already dead, that every moment he drew breath was because his father allowed it.

"I—we need the staff."

"We?" Ebon narrowed his gaze. "Do you mean my son? Has your magic made you mad?" He laughed again. "How rich! Tell me, please," he asked in an amused tone, "who else is it you speak for? Could it be your sister? I was told you'd killed her. Ironic, that. After all your efforts, all your scheming, your bargains and betrayals. So much death to save her life, yet you kill her yourself."

What is he talking about? Stone was beginning to grow more frustrated than afraid. Ebon was behaving as if they'd known each other, yet Stone was certain they'd never met. *It's possible mother told him about Willow, but what's all the other nonsense he's going on about?*

"I didn't kill her," Stone said. "Willow is still alive."

Ebon clucked his tongue. "I see. And here I thought you would've kept the artifacts for yourself. How good of you to share. But then you always were the good brother. And why is it the two of you need the staff now? You forfeited any right to do magic long ago."

"No," Stone said. *I forfeited?* "Not to do magic. To plant a new Word Tree. The staff is still alive. It's the only piece left of what you—of what's been lost. With a new Tree," he reasoned, trying to persuade his father, "the forests would grow back. The lands would become fertile. The air would return in strength. We could undo all the destruction, breathe life back into Eralle."

Stone had watched his father as he spoke, hoping for any sign he'd been convincing. Ebon no longer looked as amused, but neither did he seem swayed.

"No."

Stone blinked.

"I don't understand," Stone said, searching for any sign of emotion within his father. How could he be so uncaring? "You don't want to restore the world? You *intended* to burn it all away? For everyone to starve? For what remained to choke on the ashes?"

Ebon moved dangerously close, eyes flashing with sudden anger.

"I *intended* to be free," he said, "and will remain so until the end. You don't fool me. You have a Warden." Ebon took a step forward. "I will not be enslaved again."

"It's not like that," Stone said quickly. He bowed his head but refused to step back. "Crier is a good person. He would never do that."

Ebon swatted Stone aside, sent him sprawling across the floor. All sense erupted into a void of sound and color and hazy trembles. His father kept talking angrily. The muted words went straight through. Stone struggled to clear his sense, to get his claws back beneath him. A tail swipe sent him crashing to a wall, broken with the rocks. He wanted to speak, to calm his father, but his jaw had been shattered.

Fey magic unfurled into a chorus of harsh whisper. Willow grappled their father with a roar, swung her tail for momentum and threw him to one side. Ebon was no doubt larger, but she moved with a crazed fury. Crier ran to Stone, face strained with worry. He slid to Stone on both knees and hugged him below an eye. Healing magic was warming through before Stone could even manage to feel relief that the boy was alright.

"You would challenge me?" Ebon said in bemused disbelief. "I know the secret to your healing. Surrender to me now, or I will tear it from your chest."

Willow roared in anguished defiance. Fired spittle dripped from her maw as she charged at her father. She slid beneath his clawed attack and swiped across his middle. She lacked his utter strength but was practiced in battle. Willow chose her attacks. She screamed in rage and anger, but every claw strike, every tail swipe was delivered with precision. She breathed fire in his eyes. She used his size and weight against him, struck when he overreached, caused him to falter time and again. She used the walls to her advantage, baited him into attacks that hurt himself against the rocks. But for all her guile and exacting tactics, Willow was outmatched. Though Ebon landed one in five attacks, each claw across her scales, each tail swipe that struck true came at a devastating cost.

"Just stay still," Crier said to Stone and continued to heal his wounds. "We'll help her in a moment."

No, Stone thought in horror, watched his sister take the brunt of attacks that would have felled any other dragon. *She won't last. I have to help her now.* He looked at Crier as if it might be his last. *No matter the cost.*

Stone growled up the courage to stand, ignoring the boy's protests. He roared and took wing, flew to the top of the cavern and swung wide. With all his strength, he turned his body and dove. All four claws extended, Stone crashed into Ebon's head and dug in. He tumbled over, raked across scales and pulled down. Willow pounced at the opening, striking repeatedly with both claws across their father's neck.

"Stop!" Crier yelled. Airlings swirled into being as rocklings pulled free of the floor and walls. "All of you, stop!"

Ebon regained his balance as Willow reared for a mighty strike. He growled and moved too quick, plunged a claw through her chest. Past scale and bone, he pulled free her heart. With a satisfied huff, he let it fall to her feet.

"Willow!" Stone cried, held fast at the neck beneath a back claw. "No!"

His sister stumbled back, looking down in tearful shock. She fell over, all her anger drained away. She looked at her brother, saw him in danger and reached out to help.

Willow collapsed and moved no more.

Stone was overcome with grief and rage but unable to move. All his world, his true heart, had been torn from him. His sister was gone, truly gone, and at the moment, nothing else seemed to matter.

"Call them back," Ebon warned, "or I'll kill him too."

Crier's nostrils flared in anger. He let out a breath, unclenched his fists and let go every conjure.

"Don't hurt him."

Ebon was breathing heavy from his exertion. He was wounded in a dozen places, scales torn and bones broken.

"You care so much for a dragon?" he asked. "Come. Surrender yourself to me, and I will let him live. You have my word."

Crier stepped forward and knelt before the ancient dragon. He was afraid but firm in his resolve to save Stone. Ebon let go his hold of Stone and put a talon to Crier's neck. Willow's blood marred his skin.

"You could command me to let you go," he tempted the young Warden. "I'd have no choice but to obey."

Crier would only look at Stone.

"I would never take the free will of a living creature."

"What then?" Ebon asked, incredulous. "You would let me kill you, to save a *dragon*?"

"He's not just a dragon," Crier said and smiled. "He's my friend. I would do anything for him."

Ebon was quiet as he considered, looked to his son and the only living human left on Eralle.

"Perhaps there is hope then." He removed his talon from Crier's neck, reached into his maw and pulled free a wooden length from the side. He handed Crier the High Warden's staff. "Be a better Warden than those before you." He gave Stone a meaningful glance. "I defeated you all once. I can do it again." He moved toward the cavern tunnel and called back, "Don't be here when I return."

Crier stood as Ebon left. He looked down at his hands, where he held the last living piece of the World Tree. He placed it beside Willow and walked over to comfort Stone. He hugged his friend in the numbing quiet, offered warmth in the growing cold.

"I'm so sorry," was all he said.

Words would never be enough.

- 18 -

Stone was numb. He couldn't move, nor did he want to. It felt as if a hole had been torn in his existence, an empty void of cold and uncaring that could never again be filled. He stared at her heart. Mottled white and red, riddled by shreds and holes long before it had been torn free. Crier got up and walked over to it.

"I know it isn't any consolation," he said and reached a hand toward it, hesitant to touch, "but she was dying. All that time spent in the spirit world...she didn't have much time left. I think she knew that. It was only the Life Stones that allowed her to use the ring for as long as she did."

It was as big as he was, and when Crier touched it, the heart crumbled. It broke apart into flakes of white ash that became wisps of ghostly smoke. Her entire body followed suit but did not disappear. She remained, as a spirit, and stood before her brother.

Willow lowered her head to Stone's, touched against it with love as they'd done when they were young. She put a claw to his heart. When she spoke, her voice was like an echo of warmth reaching out to fill the void in his being.

"I will always be here," she said. "Do not forget."

Then she was gone.

All that remained of her were the life stones where her heart had been, two amber shards no bigger than snowflakes, and the spirit ring just beyond. Crier picked them up. There was no surprise in the discovery.

"How?" Stone asked. He stood for a closer look at the amber flakes in Crier's hand. "What were they doing in her heart?" *That's what healed her,* he then realized. "Does that mean I—"

The thought was cut short by an all too familiar presence. It stalked up the tunnel toward them with the blood of an eonyx in her mouth. Stone couldn't fathom why she was there. She'd left no mark upon the range or in the lair. Yet she hunted the mountains? She brought meat back to *him*? Stone rushed to guard Crier as his mother entered the cavern.

She tossed aside the eonyx. It was a large creature, similar to a goat, with twisting horns and long black fur. It was nearly half as large as Stone, yet she'd thrown it like it was nothing. Blood dripped from her maw, and there was murder in her eyes.

"I don't care what bargain you've struck," she told Stone as she approached, each step a promise of death. "My part is long done. And now, so are you."

Her hatred for him was like a palpable force, like a rising dread up from his middle that threatened to choke the life from him. All he could ask, all he ever wanted to know, was *why*? She was his mother! She should have loved him, without condition, no matter how much he displeased her. Every failed test or disappointment he'd caused was like a talon in his heart. It made it all the more difficult for her to love him. He loved her, even when every fiber of his being screamed he shouldn't, yet she refused to give him or Willow the slightest bit of affection.

Why!?

He didn't know how to activate the Warden circlet on his wing talon, to force his mother to answer truthfully, but when he opened his mouth to speak, he felt its magic come to life.

"Why do you *hate* me so?"

His voice was torn with emotion, a lifetime of pain showing through. She halted, suddenly afraid, confused and struggling with her own feelings.

"You killed my son!" she roared back.

Stone balked. "I *am* your son!"

"No!" She shook her head, growled and backed away from him in fear. "I don't know how you're still able to do magic. Just stay away from me!"

She turned and fled from the cavern. Stone stood in the wake of her tirade, more confused than ever. Crier put a hand to his leg, a cooling touch in a storm of conflicting emotions.

"Close your eyes," the boy said, "I have something to show you."

* * *

Jacoben carried with him the High Warden's staff as he entered Eboncall's lair. Lewellen wouldn't need it, not once the plan was underway. The ancient dragon flared his wings, postured as if it mattered.

"You dare enter here alone?"

The Low Warden couldn't help but feel a twinge of fear. He was, after all, only human. He looked up at the creature with forced calm.

"You are the oldest," Jacoben said, "the strongest of your kind, yet I could end you on a whim."

Eboncall snarled, thrashed in a frenzied tantrum, but did not attack. Fiery gobs flew from his maw in all directions. A few drops would have struck the Warden and burned straight through him if it weren't for the magical barrier that protected him. Light flared blue in the air where spittle struck against the magic.

"Dragons." Jacoben had said it like an insult. "So cunning, yet brutish, as like to solve your problems with claw and fire than anything else. Have you ever considered using the intellect we gave you?"

Eboncall settled his demeanor but still seethed behind his eyes.

"Why have you come?"

"To strike a bargain, of course." The length of wood tapped out against the floor as he walked a slow circle about the dragon. "You wish to be free of us, of the Maker's bond that ties you? I can do this, for a price."

Ebon glowered. "And what might that price be?"

"My sister is dying," Jacoben said, "and no potion or spell can cure her. You have offspring about to hatch. You will allow me to transfer my sister's and my spirit into two of them."

"I care nothing for your sister," the dragon said, "or any other human." Jacoben gave him a few moments to consider. With narrowed eyes, Ebon asked, "What would happen to my hatchlings?"

Jacoben chuckled. He'd already won.

"They'll be fine," the Warden lied, "sharing a body for all eternity."

In truth, the hatchling spirits would die the moment Jacoben completed the ritual. The dragon gave it more thought, shook his head as he fought against the instinct to guard his young.

"And you will betray your own," Ebon asked, "kill the other two to set us free?" He sounded disbelieving and rightfully so. No Warden had ever betrayed another. "The Tree will choose others to replace you."

"True," Jacoben said, confident in his manipulation, "but you'll have plenty of time before they're grown to find and deal with all three. You and all your kind will be free." At Ebon's scoff, the Warden added, "Tamara is my twin sister, and they refuse to do what is necessary to save her life. I do this for her and her alone."

"And yet," the dragon derided, "you include yourself in the bargain."

"Someone must look after her. She's a frail spirit, after all." Jacoben stopped and faced him, put steel in his voice. "You have eleven eggs. You will select the strongest male and female. Then you will destroy the rest."

"What!" Ebon wheeled, stalked through the cavern shaking his head in bridled anger. "I will do no such thing."

"Your mate will care for us," Jacoben continued, paid no heed to the display, "and no one else. There will be no favorites, no culling of the weak. Stormcry will care for us, teach us to survive, for no less than five years. If you do not adhere to our agreement, follow it to the letter, my tampering with the Maker's bond will come undone."

"Lies! You promised to free us of the bond!"

"And I will," Jacoben soothed, "so long as you hold true to our agreement. Magic is not *something to be trifled with."*

He played on the dragon's instinctive fear of the mysterious force that had brought their kind into being. The Wardens who had created dragons intended that fear to be one of many controls over the dangerous creatures. Another was that they could be bound by their own words.

Eboncall stopped his pacing. He'd weighed the awful bargain and decided a course.

"It will be done," the dragon agreed, "but be warned. If you do not keep your end of our accord, I will torment you and your sister for all time."

"Of course." Jacoben gave a stiff nod. "I'd expect

nothing less. Now, say the words."

Eboncall flared his nostrils with another snarl but relented in the end. Through gritted teeth, he spoke their bargain.

"I will select the strongest male and female eggs" he said, gouging talons into the rock as he spoke, "and destroy the others. My mate, Stormcry, will care for these two for no less than five years."

"Alright then," Jacoben said with a wide smile, "we both have work to do."

* * *

Stone buckled beneath the weight of realization. His father may have burned the World Tree, may have led to the extinction of humanity, but it was Stone who had set it all in motion.

"It was me," he said, voice broken, overwhelmed by loss and crushing guilt. "I'm the traitor Warden, the one who set dragons loose upon the world." He closed tight his eyes, but the tears came anyway. "I thought I'd be the one to set right all their wrongs. Instead, my legacy is ash."

"You didn't know." Crier tried to comfort him, but to Stone's ears it sounded as if he was trying to convince himself. "You couldn't know what he'd do."

"Oh, I must've thought I was so clever," Stone said, self-loathing rising up within, "outwitting Ebon, stealing lives, committing murder, the whole time thinking it would all return to normal once the new Wardens were grown. That I'd be free of my crimes, because I wouldn't remember them." He swallowed hard, nearly choked on the regrets. "And for what? My sister? The one I'd *still* do anything for." He shook his head against the terrible truth echoing through his mind. "What's worse...I don't know that I'd do anything different."

"I don't believe that for an instant," Crier said, his own voice growing heated. "You made a mistake, many horrible mistakes, for love, but that person is gone. You are *not* Jacoben! You stopped being him the moment your egg hatched." He grabbed hold of Stone's face, made Stone look him in the eyes. "The person you are now still loves just as strong. You'd do anything for your sister, for me, for Glim, but not at the expense of innocent lives. Now we can sit here and grieve and wallow over all that's been lost, or we can get up and do what we set out to do from the very beginning. You are Stonefall, and you will be remembered for the rest of time as the dragon who saved the world."

Stone wanted to believe it, to take comfort in the thought, but his guilt was too strong. He didn't deserve to be consoled, let alone forgiven.

"You have the staff," Stone said, "and a Life Stone. You don't need me."

"Of course I need you," the boy said with a chuckle. "You don't expect me to *walk* to the Wall? We've come so far together. You're my family. I will always need you. Besides," he added, "only dragons can reach the top of the Wall. There's no other way. You're just going to have to save the world and be a hero, whether you like it or not."

He knew the boy was playing, doing all he could to bring a little light to a dark situation. Stone took in a deep breath and let it out with resignation. He still felt unbearable guilt, would never get over the loss of Willow, but he did feel a sense of ease that the Tree could now be restored.

"I do love you, you know." It was the first time Stone had said it aloud. He stood and lowered his neck for the boy to climb. He'd never again be the same, but he was at least ready to put things right. “Why is it only dragons can reach the top?”

Crier hopped up and settled in, taking hold of the silken reins.

“Interesting story, actually,” he said as Stone headed out the tunnel. “When King Boris led his army to claim the Tree’s magic for his own, they only managed to chip away five small shards from the Spirit Stone before the Tree fought back. None of them survived. In their great wisdom,” Crier said with sarcasm, “the Wardens at the time cracked the land, caused it to rise and create a massive wall that cut off access to the Tree.”

“That makes no sense,” Stone said, more than aware he was being distracted. “The Wall only cuts off the north end of the continent. There’s ocean on either side. An army could simply sail around.”

“The Tree is at the bottom of the slope,” Crier said, “on the other side of the Wall. That land is surrounded by water, and it’s completely hidden by magic.” The boy shrugged. “I understand why they made the Wall, as a show of power to all the kingdoms, but if it were up to me, I would’ve just hidden the Tree on all sides by the same magic.”

“Maybe,” Stone agreed, “but magic is unreliable. A solid wall of earth that reaches into the clouds?” He gave a slight snicker. “That’s fairly reliable and a constant reminder to all who see it.”

Crier continued to tell stories of Eralle’s past as they flew. From the magicians’ rebellion to the dying of magic among humans, all the wonders of the Warden reliquary to the destruction and loss of culture caused by wars, the boy refused to let Stone be alone with his thoughts. Days later, they stopped in Oasthold to inform Durden they’d found a Life Stone. A celebration was underway in short order. They stayed for a quick rest but continued on at first light. They were both relieved and delighted upon returning home to find Glim was already there.

"You're back!" she cried with glee. She dropped her book and flew toward them, hugged each in turn. "I have so much to tell you." Her eyes widened at the length of wood fastened to Stone's back. "You did it! You got the staff! Tell me everything."

The dryad was there as well. He looked well rested, renewed and happy within the forest. He waved at their arrival but continued tending to the trees.

Crier held Glim's hand as they walked. "I'm so glad to see you again. We were both very worried."

"Really," she said and looked back at Stone as he followed after, "both of you?"

Stone bowed his head in acquiescence.

"Just a little," he admitted.

"Is it alright," Crier asked, "if I go see how Notch is doing? You can tell me all about the shadwens tonight, before we see them again tomorrow."

Glim asked, "Tomorrow?"

"We have everything we need," Stone explained and settled down to rest outside Crier's tree.

The boy smiled and held out a hand, showed her the amber shards.

"We're heading for the Wall," he said, "and tomorrow we restore the World Tree."

– 19 –

The journey north into the shadow of the Wall took less than a day. Actually reaching the raised layer of earth would take longer. It was disconcerting, to say the least, to see and feel the sun directly overhead while all around was completely shrouded in darkness. Crackles of violet sparked the edge of every rock jutting up from snow and ice, every petrified tree and crystal monolith passing beneath them. Whispers clouded the very air with a heady mist of purple white. Their voices were a mixture of young and old, male and female, fey and Warden and many others Stone didn't know. It was as if the land itself was alive with magic, an amalgam of countless years absorbing spells and enchantments across its surface. While the magic was loud, demanded his attention, it didn't scare him like the shadwens.

And they were on him in short order.

They scrabbled across the snow on all fours as beasts and feys. Through amethyst glow and glint, across the crackles they shifted. Some with wings, some as spirits, they rose into the air. True shapeshifters all, they weren't bound to the same form as Glim when she walked in shadow. They came at Stone with purpose and carried with them the intense dread he'd felt back at the forest. He nearly froze in air but for her voice reaching his ear.

"Keep going," Glim told him. "It will be alright."

She stood and held tight to a spine upon his neck, shifted into shadow and called out a welcome murmur. Each gathered round her to touch a shoulder, spreading chill across Stone's back.

"They're amazing," Crier said, watching them speak together from his perch beside her.

"Yes," Stone said unconvincingly, struggling to keep his anxiety from upending breakfast fruit, "amazing."

The shadwens broke off and flew ahead with dizzying speed. Glim shifted and tied herself back into place beside Crier.

"They'll all know we're coming soon." She'd said it as a reassurance, but all it did was bolster Stone's panic. "We can rest at any crystal and be safe."

Just how many of them are there? Stone thought of the cursed shifters. The trees here were all dead. There were no plants or grass. *What exactly are they feeding on?*

"What are the crystals?" Crier asked and leaned over the side for a better look. "I thought I saw one just a bit ago. Are they natural?"

"There's so much magic here," Glim explained, "that it leaves residue in the air. Shadwens gather it to brace or build new shelters. Each monolith is home to dozens of shadwens."

One came into sense as they passed over a frozen pond. It jutted up through snow the length of a talon. Like a pillar of shaped violet, salted ice in swirling black, it was the focus of a group of shadwens standing guard about its base.

"When they need to rest," Glim continued, "they can shift inside the crystal. It sustains them when they can't find any food. If we need to stop, it's best we do so near a monolith. They promised to help protect us while we rest."

Stone sensed nothing else but shadwens, though the magic permeating all was like a blanket over his head. It dulled his sense, muffled every input.

"What else is out here?" Stone asked and brought them higher above the snow.

Glim quickly said, "No. Stay as low to the ground as you can. There are tainted ursals and canin packs, but it's the pallors we need to watch for."

Crier shivered. "Do I even want to know?"

"It's part of the curse," Glim replied. "Shadwens can only die by violence. When that happens, it becomes a pallor, an angry spirit that feeds on life and the light of a full moon."

Stone grumbled. Could it be that aspect of them that causes such intense dread within him?

"Can they be killed?" he asked.

"Not by a shadwen," Glim said, lowered her head and voice, "and not by me. Only a pure fey can strike down a pallor. We can try to harm them," she added, "if we have to. It's just very dangerous."

"We won't," Stone said firmly. "Better to fly off than risk fighting a spirit. The shadwens can hide inside their crystals. If we see a pallor, we flee. Agreed?"

Both nodded in somber quiet. Though the mood had been dampened, they were drawing closer to their goal. In two more days, it wouldn't matter. They'd reach the base of the Wall and could leave behind the chilling dark.

By the time they'd stopped to rest, Stone had sensed and avoided a tainted ursal outside its rocky den. The creature's fur had the same crackling violet to its sheen as every other magic-infused facet of the land. Its eyes had glowed a bright purple and its spittle a sickly green.

What it hunted to survive was a mystery to Stone. Could shadwens be eaten? He shivered in disgust. As hungry as he was, Stone had no intention of ingesting a creature that had been corrupted by magic. He'd left behind the tainted ursal, long accustomed to his own hunger.

The night passed without trouble, long hours in the quiet dark. It wasn't until their next night at rest, while being visited by Glim's grandfather, that their peace was interrupted.

It came wailing across the snow, like a shriek of graying white. Tattered clothes, shorn flesh, skeletal face and violet eyes, the pallor looked like a long dead fey had clawed its way up from the ground. It had no physical form, just a ghostly torso and dirtied silk where its legs should have been. The snow beneath it blackened but didn't melt, as if ash had spread across the top. The grating stench of death and decay billowed out from its body like a tangible force. Mouth agape, bony fingers out like claws, it sped toward them with a jealous craving for their lives.

"Crier!" Stone shouted. "Glim! To me!"

He was up in an instant, gauging the distance and ready to flee. They scrambled to climb his neck, as a host of shadwens rushed to head off the shrieking pallor. He didn't wait for them to sit securely in place or tie off with silken strands. Once he felt them upon his scales, Stone turned north and moved to leave.

"Wait!" Glim cried. "Grandpa, no!"

The pallor had taken hold of her grandfather by the neck. Though he struggled to pull free, though others struck with shadow blade, he could not break the bony grasp. Golden light erupted from beneath its touch, as if the pallor had torn him open and revealed the sunlight deep within. It drew in his essence, brightening its own grayish glow to white.

Glim was down before Stone could take another step. She took wing toward the snow and shifted onto ground. Shadow dagger in hand, she charged the vengeful spirit. Her frantic whisper rose above the others, a desperate plea to free her kin.

Crier leapt down with staff in hand. The snow went past his knees, made it difficult to run. He struggled to reach the fray, called airlings in his wake. Stone growled and turned to rush after.

"Glim!" Crier called out, as if knowing he'd never get to her in time. Their shadow blades did little damage. In only a matter of moments her grandfather would be no more. "Catch!"

He tossed her the High Warden staff.

Glim had been railing against the pallor to no effect. It refused to loosen its grip, had nearly drained all his light. Her shadow turned in time to see the staff arcing in air. She shifted back and caught it, swung it hard in one swift motion. It struck against the pallor and exploded in raucous silver. Like a flash of moonlight in its bones, beneath the dead flesh, the strike had touched deep into the heart of the angry spirit. Glim drove the staff forward into the pallor's middle. Great flash after another, she forced it to set free her grandfather and drove it back from all the others. A final thrust with all her might, and the staff went straight through its chest. Ghostly light pulsed within its ribcage, faster and faster until the pallor dissipated into a shock of dying light.

Trembling, Glim dropped to her knees. Crier made it to her side and put an arm around her. Other shadwen gathered to aid her grandfather.

"How?" she asked and looked down at her shaking hands. "I'm not a pure fey."

Crier put a hand to his heart.

"In here," he told her. When she looked up into his

gaze, he tapped his chest again for emphasis.

Glim couldn't help but smile.

* * *

They reached the Wall at midday. It towered above, stretched far into dark clouds and the sparks of violet storm. Rock and earthen striations were clearly visible as they rose, clear marks of where the mantle had been torn and forced upward. The whispers grew more intense the higher they flew, swirled a chorus in the clash of thunder and unbridled gale. Stone worried for Glim and Crier, though they were securely tied in place. The steep ascent and jarring wind threatened to pull them from his back. The air was growing thinner as well. It became difficult to fill his lungs. They didn't burn from exertion, as they had when he crossed the marsh. There just wasn't enough to sustain him, left him shaking and out of breath.

If other dragons truly did fear magic, the fact Ebon had made this climb was a testament to his conviction. All sight had been lost to mist, a clouded clamor of voices chanting out their sullen murmurs. They tried to frighten him off, sent ghostly visages to assail him. When Stone persisted, they tried to misdirect, showed images of the Wall further off to the south. But dragons didn't need eyes to see. He could feel the Wall's presence against the hairs between his scales, kept track of its passing with the barest touch of tail and claw.

No magic could trick the senses of a dragon.

When they finally crested the top, they had left the mist behind. Its whispers fell away and were replaced by sun's embrace. The World Tree came into view at the same moment. They headed down the slope of barren soil and upended rock. Up ahead, unlike any other they'd ever seen, the Tree stood as tall as a small mountain.

Its trunk spread so wide before them, it was like another living Wall. Thousands of dragons, wing to wing, could have rounded its base with room to spare. Its roots were as big as heartwoods, twisted up and knotted down deep into earth. Its branches filled the sky, stretched to the clouds and from one end of the horizon to the other. While the larger boughs were up top, there were smaller ones all the way down.

Straight up its center, the Tree was cracked, split open and laid bare. The blackened divide caused by Ebon's heart of fire had destroyed its Spirit Stone, ate away all its center, down into the soil. Withered, broken, long dead by malice, its remains were but a shadow of the splendor it once was.

They flew toward the break.

"It's magnificent," Crier said, "and heartbreaking at the same time."

Stone remained silent. His part in its destruction was all too clear in his mind. Nothing he could say would warrant his forgiveness or alleviate his guilt. All he could do from that moment on was strive to be better.

Glim put a hand to Crier's shoulder in consolation.

"It will be beautiful again," she promised.

Stone landed before the opening, where the Spirit Stone was once housed. Its amber was no more. All that remained was a hollow, like the half of an eggshell. Crier walked inside and knelt, placed a shard within the ash of the concave. He reached out with the staff and touched it to the remnants of thin roots beyond the shard's reach. The staff bridged the gap, and in that instant came alive. From amber shard to blackened root, a flash of emerald life spread outward. Roots stretched like fingers, grew to encase the amber. It now pulsed like a heartbeat within the chest of the World Tree.

"We did it," Crier said in wonder, looked up to see life

returning to the Tree. "We did it!"

He jumped up and ran to Stone, who lowered his head to endure a hug. Even he felt a lifting of the gloom that had haunted him and smiled at the marvel taking place right before them. Glim joined in their embrace, kissed Stone upon his maw.

"I never doubted you for a moment," she said, "either of you." She stepped back and craned her neck, watched life slowly returning to the bark and every branch. "What will happen next?"

Stone felt a rush of clean air rise up to touch his face. He took in a deep breath of it, felt his lungs fill with promise.

"The land will heal," he said and exhaled. He felt relief in that moment, a true sense of ease he didn't think possible before. "We'll make sure of it."

In the days that came and went, they tended to the Tree. They helped clear away fallen branches and moved rocks from inside the chamber. There was a warmth about the trunk that melted snow and cleansed the soil. A dried river bed returned to life, carried to them clear and sweet water. As they worked to do all they could for its needs, the Tree in turn provided for them. New fruits and nuts sprouted from the lower branches. Buds opened, leaves spread and all came alive with the colors of spring.

From two of the lower branches, a wooden egg had appeared on each. They were similar to Crier's but much smaller. Stone pointed them out and wondered aloud just what they were—or would one day be.

"Wardens," Crier replied. He looked up at them and was happy. "I'll have to give up two of my gifts, but it will be worth it for the extra company."

Far above, in the higher branches, hundreds more were taking shape.

"And those?" Stone asked, indicating the new eggs.

The boy craned his neck and squinted, as if he could barely see that far. He looked back at Stone and winked, laughed at the dragon's puzzled look.

"Another gift," Crier said, "promise of a new future."

☼☼☼

About the Author

A Fantasy and Science Fiction author with numerous short stories and books published in many formats and read worldwide, J.A. Giunta has a B.A. in English from Arizona State and has worked in the IT industry for over 15 years. He makes appearances at conventions and events, including Tucson Festival of Books and Phoenix Comicon. He lives in the perpetual summer that is central Arizona and can be found online at jagiunta.com.

Manufactured by Amazon.ca
Bolton, ON

20065043R00118